KV-336-087

NURSE OF SPIRIT LAKE

NURSE OF SPIRIT LAKE

DOROTHY BRENNER FRANCIS

THORNDIKE
CHIVERS

This Large Print edition is published by Thorndike Press, Waterville, Maine USA and by BBC Audiobooks Ltd, Bath, England.

Thorndike Press is an imprint of Thomson Gale, a part of The Thomson Corporation.

Thorndike is a trademark and used herein under license.
Copyright © 1975 by Dorothy Brenner Francis.

The moral right of the author has been asserted.

ALL RIGHTS RESERVED

The text of this Large Print edition is unabridged.

Other aspects of the book may vary from the original edition.
Set in 16 pt. Plantin.

LIBRARY OF CONGRESS CATALOGING-IN-PUBLICATION DATA

Francis, Dorothy Brenner.
  Nurse of Spirit Lake / by Dorothy Brenner Francis.
    p. cm. — (Thorndike Press large print candlelight.)
  ISBN-13: 978-0-7862-9307-0 (alk. paper)
  ISBN-10: 0-7862-9307-1 (alk. paper)
  1. Nurses — Fiction. 2. Aunts — Fiction. 3. Lodging-houses — Fiction. 4. Spirit Lake (Iowa) — Fiction. 5. Large type books. I. Title.
PS3556.R327N86845 2007
813'.54—dc22   2006035373

BRITISH LIBRARY CATALOGUING-IN-PUBLICATION DATA AVAILABLE

Published in 2007 in the U.S. by arrangement with Maureen Moran Agency.
Published in 2007 in the U.K. by arrangement with the author.

U.K. Hardcover: 978 1 405 64020 6 (Chivers Large Print)
U.K. Softcover: 978 1 405 64021 3 (Camden Large Print)

Printed in the United States of America on permanent paper
10 9 8 7 6 5 4 3 2 1

KENT
ARTS & LIBRARIES
C152909184

For Janey Montgomery, who suggested
the setting for this story

CHAPTER ONE

Ellen Ferris slowed her Volkswagen, easing it through the sleeping village of Spirit Lake. With the exception of two overnight stops she had driven steadily from California to Iowa, and now she felt a desire to slow down. She needed to gather her thoughts before she faced Aunt Madeleine.

A full June moon silvered the old-fashioned brick and frame homes set in emerald-green lawns along Main Street, but Ellen hardly noticed them as she headed toward the blacktop north of town. Soon she saw a sign advertising Scarlet Point Lodge on Big Spirit Lake, Madeleine Ferris owner and operator.

Ellen thought of Aunt Madeleine's recent telephone call. For as long as Ellen had known her, Aunt Madeleine never had been one to write letters. Letters gave a person a chance to think, a chance to refuse unpopular requests. Ellen sighed. She was being unfair. She hadn't wanted to refuse Aunt Madeleine's request to come to Scarlet Point. In fact, she had welcomed the invitation. It had come at an opportune time; school was out and she needed to get away from her teaching responsibilities at the hospital. Her problems with Janey Van Allen, Mr. Van Allen, and the board of directors at the nursing school were getting her down. A respite at Scarlet Point would give her time to think and perhaps decide the best line of action to take.

Ever since Ellen's parents had died when she was fifteen, Aunt Madeleine had been generous with her — on her own terms, of course. She had kept Ellen in good boarding schools and excellent summer camps; then she had sponsored her professional education on the agreement that Ellen would enter nursing school. Aunt Madeleine had played deaf when Ellen had said she wanted to be a teacher. But Ellen's schooling had worked out to everyone's satisfaction. Ellen enjoyed her position teaching in the Mercedes School of Nursing in California. She felt deeply indebted to Aunt Madeleine.

An opossum waddling across the blacktop toward a cornfield focused Ellen's attention on the present. She braked the car to avoid hitting the animal, then drove on even more slowly. As she rounded a bend in the road, Scarlet Point Lodge loomed brooding and massive on her right. Ellen turned onto a short lane leading under a towering white archway that was topped with a red tile roof. Broken coach lights hung from either side of the arch, and the white-painted iron gates sagged open, one completely off its hinges, the other leaning at a crazy angle.

Ellen drove through the archway, then stopped for a moment in awe. Scarlet Point Lodge seemed a block long, and its U-shaped frame rose four stories high. Moonlight glinted on the red tile roof and the Spanish belfry towers with their Gothic arches. An owl flew from one belfry, silhouetting itself against the moon. Its eerie cry made Ellen shiver.

Ellen glanced at her watch. Midnight. Perhaps she should have stayed in a motel in Spirit Lake and waited until morning to make her appearance at the lodge. But no. Someone was awake. Ellen watched for a moment as a beam of light flashed across an upper room then vanished. She straightened her shoulders. She was here. Aunt Madeleine was expecting her. She would knock at the front door.

Three cars sat like stage props in a huge

parking lot at the side of the lodge, but Ellen drove past them and parked at the main entrance to the lodge. Grass grew through cracks in the cement driveway. Foxtail and thistles almost hid a wrought-iron sundial on the front lawn. An orange fire hydrant seemed totally out of place near a rural mailbox, but at least someone had mowed around these.

Although the June night was warm, Ellen clamped her jaws together to keep her teeth from chattering. What had Aunt Madeleine been thinking of when she bought a run-down lodge like this? Ellen recalled a family comment to the effect that guessing what Aunt Madeleine was up to was like trying to rehearse the unexpected. She agreed, but she tried to keep an open mind.

Sliding from the car, Ellen walked to the door of the lodge. She could see no doorbell, so she knocked. No answer. She rapped again and pressed her forehead against the window glass as she peered into the dark interior. After a long wait a light flashed on deep inside the cavernous building. Another light flashed on. Then another. Presently the door creaked open and Aunt Madeleine stood framed in the entryway.

"Ellen!" With bracelets ajangle and ruffled sleeves flowing, Aunt Madeleine swooped upon Ellen, wrapping her in an enthusiastic hug. Then, holding Ellen at arm's length, she smiled. "You haven't changed a bit. I'd have known that brown hair and those blue eyes anywhere. And that stubborn Ferris chin. So you're here at last!"

"It's good to be here," Ellen said, slipping the words into her aunt's flow of conversation.

"I've looked for you all day long." Aunt Madeleine stepped back. "Do come inside and I'll make us some hot chocolate. We can get your things later."

Ellen inhaled the scent of English lavender that was her aunt's trademark. "Thank you, Aunt Madeleine. That would be nice. I'm sorry to come barging in here in the middle of the night, but —"

"Don't apologize, child. I couldn't sleep for wondering and worrying about you making that long drive all alone. Come along, now."

Ellen came along. Like most wealthy women, Aunt Madeleine expected obedience, expected the world to conform to her plans. Although Ellen hadn't seen her aunt for over three years, she hadn't changed. Even at midnight in a run-down lodge Aunt Madeleine gave the impression of being a frivolous glamor girl.

Aunt Madeleine was tall and thin. She always referred to herself as willowy, but to Ellen her aunt was tall and thin. She wore her blue-gray hair in an upsweep with soft curls framing her face. She always painted her mouth into a Cupid's bow, and even now, at midnight, she wore mascara and eye liner. Her lavender jersey robe had ruffles at the neck, the sleeves, the hem. Aunt Madeleine was a whipped-cream sort of person who always reminded Ellen of a nineteenth-century valentine — all frills and lace and surprises. Ellen was glad she took after her mother's side of the family. She didn't mind being big-boned and a bit too tall, and after twenty-five years of living she decided that her straight, blunt-cut hair suited her. She was nothing like Aunt Madeleine.

"Did you have a good trip?" Aunt Madeleine asked, setting a cup of instant hot chocolate in front of her niece.

"Very pleasant. I always enjoy driving." Ellen sipped her drink and glanced around the room. The high-ceilinged kitchen with its tiled floor seemed cold and forbidding. Stoves and refrigerators lined one wall, and storage shelves lined another. In its heyday Scarlet Point Lodge must have been quite a showplace.

"Aunt Madeleine, what are you trying to do here? You told me you were operating a lake lodge, but I hadn't expected anything as large as this. It's . . . it's overwhelming."

"The lodge is a bit spacious, isn't it? But I'm not attempting to operate it on a full-scale basis. Not this summer, at least." A faraway look filled Aunt Madeleine's eyes as she continued. "Your uncle Brad and I always summered here at Scarlet Point when he was living. You wouldn't remember; you were always off at camp. We felt you should be with people your own age. I suppose it was sentimental of me to buy the place when it came up for sale last month, but I just couldn't resist."

"You own all of this?" Ellen's teaspoon clattered into her saucer.

"Of course I own it. Paid cash. How can I expect to run a place properly unless I own it? Oh, I know what you're thinking. I know I've no knack for business, but I'll hire advisors. I'm a wealthy woman, and while I may not be able to do brainy things, I try to make up for it by doing worthwhile things with my money. I couldn't just sit by and watch this lovely old lodge decay into ruin. Brad and I were so happy here. I just know he would want me to try to keep the place going."

"How many guests do you have?" Ellen asked.

"You always drive right to the point, don't you?" Aunt Madeleine laughed. "But I guess that's what I need — someone practical at my side to keep me in line. I'll never forget you as a child, Ellen. While all the other little girls were learning to embroider tea towels, you were learning how to change blown fuses and repair leaky faucets."

"How many guests *do* you have?" Ellen repeated her question.

"Four. Or five, if you count Doug Cooper."

"Who's Doug Cooper? And why wouldn't you count him?"

"I don't count Doug as a guest because he helps out doing odd jobs in return for his room and board. Doug claims he's a writer. He always carries a clipboard with a yellow pencil tied to it, but I've never seen him writing. He's a good handyman, though. And a nice person. You two would make a handsome-looking couple."

"Who are your other guests?" Ellen asked, hoping her aunt wasn't going to play matchmaker.

Aunt Madeleine shrugged. "Well, there's Judge Cloud. He has asthma. Then there's Mrs. Young. She's just recovering from a stroke. And Miss Speer has high blood pressure. Then there's Mr. Boast."

"What's the matter with Mr. Boast?" Ellen asked.

"Not a thing. He's a retired businessman, and at age seventy-seven he jogs every morning, then breakfasts on alfalfa sprouts and basic granola."

"Are you trying to run a health farm for the aged?" Ellen asked. "With that lineup I can understand why you think you need a nurse in residence."

Aunt Madeleine offered Ellen another marshmallow for her hot chocolate. "I'm trying to save Scarlet Point Lodge from ruin and at the same time provide a nice, quiet spot where elderly people can spend a pleasant summer. And you're right — my guests are the big reason why I wanted you to come and oversee a first-aid station for me. Of course there are doctors and a hospital nearby, but I need a nurse right on the scene in case of some emergency."

"You have four guests, maybe five, and there must be two hundred rooms in this place." Ellen shook her head. "Aunt Madeleine, you're going to go broke."

"I'm no such thing. I have an architect working with me. I forgot to mention him. Frank Welborn. He's living here for the time being — likes to keep close to his work. We're going to modernize a few features — add a new heating system, install an elevator. After those things are done, I'll launch a huge advertising campaign. People will flock here. You'll see."

Ellen glanced at her watch. She was too tired to argue with her aunt or to listen to more plans. "It's almost one o'clock, Aunt Madeleine. I'd better bring in some of the things from my car and let you get to bed."

"Of course, my dear. Of course. You must be exhausted." Aunt Madeleine set their cups and saucers in the sink and led the way back to the lodge entrance. Ellen brought in one suitcase and her cosmetic case.

"May I leave my car where it is?" she asked.

"Of course. Nobody will be arriving except Josie Beanblossom, the cook, and she'll use the parking lot. Follow me. I have a bedroom all prepared for you."

Ellen followed her aunt across a parlor large enough to be a ballroom. Their heels clicked against the bare floor as they passed a grand piano and a massive fireplace. Two winding stairways with white balustrades, one on either side of the room, led to the upper floors of the lodge. Ellen glanced

16

overhead. There was no ceiling, but four floors above them a skylight framed a full moon and a scattering of stars. Scarlet Point Lodge was indeed beautiful. For a moment Ellen could understand her aunt's attachment to the place.

Aunt Madeleine stopped on the second floor and led Ellen to a large room that overlooked the lake. A braided rug was a perfect foil for the maple furniture, the chintz curtains, and the fireplace. Ellen set her suitcase on a luggage rack at the foot of the bed, and Aunt Madeleine plunked her cosmetic case down on the desk, narrowly missing a carafe of water and an empty glass.

"Now, if there's anything you want or need, just let me know," Aunt Madeleine said. "I want you to be comfortable here. Tomorrow I'll show you the rooms I've chosen for your first-aid station. They're on the first floor. I'm keeping the older guests all on the first floor for the time being. Of course, when we get the elevator installed . . ."

"Installing an elevator must be terribly expensive," Ellen said. "Shouldn't you fill the first floor with guests before you even consider adding an elevator? What if —"

"An elevator's expensive but necessary." Aunt Madeleine walked to the window and looked at the lake for a moment; then she sat down on Ellen's bed. "I've been so busy talking about me, about my interests, that I've hardly had time to think about you. You mentioned some problem in California, didn't you? Something concerning your nursing school?"

Ellen sighed. "Yes. I am having problems, but talking the night away isn't going to solve them. I don't want to keep you up any longer, Aunt Madeleine. I know you'll have lots of work to do tomorrow."

"Nonsense!" Aunt Madeleine slapped the pillow with the palm of her hand. "Now, out with it. What's troubling you in California? It must be something serious if it can send you running to Iowa."

"I'm not running." Ellen tried not to bristle.

"Sit down and tell me about it." Aunt Madeleine patted the bed beside her. "Sometimes talking a thing through helps."

Ellen sat. It was easier to obey than to argue. "There's this girl in California — Janey Van Allen. She's a student at the nursing school. I caught her cheating on an exam. There was no question about it: she was cheating. School rules require the board of directors to expel such students if the teacher requests it."

"So let them expel her." Aunt Madeleine batted her long lashes and inspected a crimson fingernail. "That doesn't seem so difficult to figure out. Even I —"

"It's not that simple." Ellen kicked off her shoes and flexed her toes. "Janey Van Allen has a wealthy father who donates generously to the hospital. If his daughter is expelled, the hospital will lose the benefit of his donation. He's made that quite clear. The hospital's small and overcrowded most of the time. It needs all the funds it can get."

"You do have a problem." Aunt Madeleine nodded. "I'm sorry I spoke so hastily."

"If I let the girl stay in school, I'll have compromised — let money outweigh integrity. If I let the board kick her out, I'll have denied the hospital needed funds and maybe blocked a promising career."

"You could resign," Aunt Madeleine suggested. "That would get you off the hook. I'll have employment for you here. I'll match whatever you were earning at the nursing school. You don't need to worry about money."

"But teaching is my thing, Aunt Madeleine. I spent years preparing for my career. If I resign I'll be out of a job, and jobs are hard to find right now. A teacher is effective only as long as she's teaching.

Anyway, I consider resigning an admission of defeat. There has to be some better way to deal with the situation."

Aunt Madeleine stood, and suddenly she looked tired. Ellen was sorry she had burdened her with nursing-school talk. Aunt Madeleine had quite enough worries of her own, problems she might be unable to solve no matter how much money she had.

"Things will look brighter in the morning," Aunt Madeleine said. "They always do. Now, you get a good night's sleep and I'll see you at breakfast. Nine o'clock. There's a bathroom right down the hall on your right. Help yourself to anything you need."

When Aunt Madeleine was gone, Ellen unpacked a few things, took a quick bath, then returned to her room and slipped into her pajamas. Was anyone else living on this floor? she wondered. Snapping off her light, Ellen stood for a moment looking down at Big Spirit Lake. Moonlight glinting on the water varnished the choppy waves with silver. Ellen wondered why the water was so rough, but she thought no more about it as she saw a light flicker along the lakeshore near the lodge. Ellen stared intently, but the screen of oak leaves below her window blocked her vision. In a moment the light

20

disappeared, and with it, her curiosity. She crawled into bed and fell asleep immediately.

CHAPTER TWO

The next morning Ellen wakened early. For a moment she lay listening to a wren trilling its song, to a redbird calling to its mate, and to blackbirds chirping and scolding. She wished she could have slept longer, but the sun flashing through her east window was a silent bugle bidding her to rise. Dressing quickly in denim shorts and a tank top, she walked quietly downstairs and outside. Nobody else was up yet, so she decided to take a stroll along the lakeshore.

Leaving the first-floor parlor by a lake-front exit, Ellen walked across a patio studded with lawn chairs and umbrella tables, then down two wide flights of cement steps that ended on a concrete quay at the water's edge. Halfway down the steps she passed a niche in the concrete retaining wall that was inset with a bench large enough for one or two people to sit to rest. Ellen passed the bench and walked on toward the lake. At the foot of the steps she broke off a leaf of fragrant spearmint from a clump of plants and sucked its tangy flavor.

The morning vibrated with sound. Blue jays scolded as she invaded their terrain. Robins chirped. Ellen saw three rabbits scamper from under an oak tree and rustle reedlike grass in a thicket near the water. For a moment she couldn't place the sound of metal clanging against metal; then she spied a flagpole with a chain slapping against the iron fastenings. Water lapping against the shoreline provided a liquid accompaniment for all the other sounds.

The breeze blowing across the water cooled Ellen's cheeks, bringing with it the sweet, pungent smell of the lake. She touched the rough bark of an elm sapling that clung to the rocky shoreline as she stooped to examine a clump of buttercups, which dotted the ground with yellow blossoms.

"Good morning."

Ellen jumped, startled. Then she turned to face a young man of medium height with sandy hair and a sprinkling of freckles across his nose and cheekbones. He carried a clipboard, and his faded brown slacks and green shirt blended with the outdoors. He had a lean, David Copperfield kind of look that made Ellen want to feed him.

"Didn't mean to startle you. I'm Doug Cooper. You must be Ellen Ferris."

"Right." Ellen smiled at Doug, liking the slow, drawling lilt of his voice. "Aunt Madeleine mentioned you last night. I'm glad she has someone here to help her out. I think she's going to need help and lots of it."

Doug chuckled, and Ellen liked the sound. His laugh matched his voice, ringing with patience and genuine humor. "Your aunt has her problems, all right, but now that you're here I'm sure things will shape up."

"You've got to be kidding." Ellen scanned Doug's face, trying to read meaning into his words. "I've just come to help her with a first-aid station. I know nothing about running a lake lodge."

"Then we'll all learn together." Doug stepped closer to Ellen. "May I join you? I like to walk along the lakeshore in the early morning."

Ellen eyed Doug's clipboard, noting that he had written nothing on it. "Be my guest, Doug. I was just going to explore for a few minutes. I saw a light down here last night, and I wondered about it. Do you walk at night, too?"

Doug shook his head. "Probably just some

die-hard fisherman. They say the catfish bite well under the full moon." Doug fell in step with Ellen, and soon they left Scarlet Point's cement retaining wall behind and strolled along the rock-strewn beach. Ellen tried to ignore a fishy smell that wafted to them on the breeze.

"Aunt Madeleine tells me that you're a writer. What do you write?"

"Novels mostly. Now and then I write articles or a few pulp stories to pick up a little cash, but mostly I work on novels."

"Are you writing one now?"

"I'm always writing. That's the beauty of being a writer. One can loaf. One can stare into space. One can doze in the sun. And if anyone comments, one can always say one is gathering material."

Ellen grinned. She liked Doug Cooper even though she sensed an unrest in him that belied his carefree words about writers and their *modus operandi*.

"Scarlet Point." Ellen turned and looked back at the lodge on the bluff above them. "I suppose the place got its name from the red tile roof."

"Good guess." Doug chuckled. "Very good guess. But not quite accurate. The lodge is really named after an old-time Sioux chief. Inkpaduta was his Indian name.

I'm not sure, but I think that translates to Scarlet Point. Inkpaduta was a bad actor. He was not just a bad Indian; he was an evil human being. Even his own people hated him."

"What did he do?" Ellen asked. "He sounds like a real doll."

"Haven't you heard of the Spirit Lake massacre? It was a sad episode in Iowa history. In the 1850s Scarlet Point led a band of Sioux that attacked the white settlers along the shore of West Okoboji Lake. There are three big lakes in this area, you know. Or maybe four, if you count Little Spirit."

"The Iowa Great Lakes," Ellen said. "East and West Okoboji and Big and Little Spirit. I've often heard Aunt Madeleine speak of them."

"Right," Doug said.

"Why did Scarlet Point lead this raid?" Ellen asked.

"Stories differ. Some say Scarlet Point was avenging his brother's death — a brother who was killed by white men. Others say that the Indians considered Big Spirit a sacred water and resented the white man's infringing into their sacred territory."

Ellen held a sapling aside as she walked nearer to the lake. "I wonder why Big Spirit was considered sacred and the other lakes weren't."

"Are you really interested?" Doug asked. "I don't want to bore you."

"Of course I'm interested. History and Indian lore always fascinate me."

"There's a legend that says the Indians believed that their Great Spirit governed the waters of Big Spirit Lake, making them rough or smiling or sad. According to the tale, there was once an island somewhere in the lake. Those who paddled too near it were seized by demons and drowned. Then one day the island disappeared, and from then on demon spirits troubled the lake waters. From that day on the Indians never floated their canoes on Big Spirit."

Ellen turned to look at Doug. "I always wonder if legends are true. They always seem fantastic, yet there's usually a grain of truth in them."

"I can't verify the legend," Doug said, "but people who live in this area claim that no Indian canoes or canoe fragments were ever found in this lake or washed up on its shores. And they also claim that Big Spirit waters are restless even when the Okobojis are calm and serene."

Ellen glanced at her watch. "I've got to get back to the lodge. Aunt Madeleine will be wondering what's happened to me."

Doug stepped up an embankment and held out his hand. "If you're in a hurry, there's a footpath up here. The going will be quicker."

Ellen took Doug's hand, and he hoisted her up onto the path. "Thanks. I really should get back quickly." Doug Cooper attracted her more than she cared to admit. He wasn't exactly handsome, yet he was nice enough looking. And there was a warmth and sincerity about him that made her feel they had been friends forever.

Doug pointed to his left. "See that cluster of oaks way over there?"

Ellen nodded.

"That's the former site of the Marble cabin. The Marbles were one of the families killed in the Spirit Lake massacre."

Ellen shuddered, turned her back on the scene, and hurried toward the lodge. When they arrived at Scarlet Point, the lodge still seemed to sleep.

"Wonder where everyone is," Ellen said.

"Except for Mr. Boast the guests are late risers. And sometimes it's just as well for your aunt to sleep. I should warn you that she has a knack for doing the wrong thing at the wrong time."

"I guessed as much from comments she

dropped last night." Ellen smiled. "Aunt Madeleine senses her shortcomings, but she means well."

"I'll try to remember that the next time she removes the extensions from the roof downspouts."

"Why did she do that?"

Doug shrugged. "She thought they looked ugly stretching out onto the lawn. And she was right; the extensions are no things of beauty. As you say, she meant well. But she didn't know that the extensions were there for a good reason. She knows now. It took us three days to mop water from the basement after the last big rain. I think the extensions will stay in place from now on."

"If you're trying to write comedy, Aunt Madeleine must be an inspiration to you."

"Comedy is not quite my line," Doug said. "I'm a serious novelist. Or at least I'm trying to be."

"But what are you doing here?" Ellen asked. "Where are you from?"

"I'm from down in Kansas. Just came here to see what there is to see. Opinions differ, but I think a writer needs to travel — while he's young, at least. I want to grow in my art, and in order to grow, one has to see things and sometimes make things happen. But I'm not fooling myself. I know that no matter how far a guy travels there's nowhere to look for subject matter except within oneself."

"I've never thought much about that," Ellen admitted. "But if you say it's so, I'll believe you."

"I'm boring you." Doug grinned. "I apologize."

"You're not boring me," Ellen said. "I enjoyed our walk, but I've got to go upstairs and finish unpacking and prepare to meet the day. Do you have breakfast with the guests?"

Doug nodded. "We all eat together. Nine o'clock. At that late hour it's more like brunch."

"I'll see you then." Ellen smiled and started up the curving stairs to the second floor. What had she got herself into? Doug had verified her suspicion that her aunt knew nothing about running a lodge. How would she ever make it through the summer? What Aunt Madeleine seemed to need more than a nurse was a good supply of common sense. Even a business advisor couldn't be constantly at hand to advise on details such as drainage downspouts.

When Ellen reached her room, she paused. Hadn't she left her door open? She distinctly remembered that she had. She had wanted to disturb nobody, so she had crept out into the hallway and left the door open. But now it was closed. As she stood considering that fact she heard noises from within.

Aunt Madeleine. Surely Aunt Madeleine was up and about and trying to be useful. Ellen felt guilty. She should have unpacked her car before taking off on a morning walk. Had Aunt Madeleine lugged her suitcases up all those stairs? Ellen opened the door. Then she stepped back in surprise. A strange man stood beside her desk, scowling at her.

CHAPTER THREE

"Who are you?" Ellen looked the stranger in the eye. "And what are you doing in my room? Does Aunt Madeleine know you're here?"

"You must be Ellen Ferris," the man said, ignoring Ellen's questions. "It's super to meet you. I hope you'll pardon this king-size intrusion. I'm Frank Welborn. Maybe your aunt mentioned me."

Ellen nodded, but she couldn't get a word in.

"I'm the chief architect who's helping her plan a more adequate heating system for the lodge." Frank smiled as he walked toward Ellen and offered his hand.

As she shook hands Ellen studied Frank Welborn. He was a sleek type who might have stepped from a clothing advertisement in a slick magazine. Ellen eyed his tailored slacks and his light-blue shoes, which exactly matched his sport shirt. She saw these things even before she noticed Frank's blond hair, his blue eyes, and his deeply suntanned skin. Frank Welborn was handsome and he had the build of a pro football player, but that still didn't explain what he was doing in her room at eight-thirty in the morning.

"Aunt Madeleine sent you up here?" Ellen asked after they had shaken hands.

"Not exactly," Frank replied. "I have the room next to yours. Your aunt has put all her agile guests on the second floor. I'm staying here for a few days while I take measurements and draw up new plans. I intended to measure your room before you arrived, but yesterday was a super-busy day. When we finally got that ocean of paint cleaned up off the front steps, it was time to knock off for the day."

"Paint?" Ellen asked, wondering if Frank always talked in superlatives.

"Black paint," Frank said, sitting down on the sturdy stones of the fireplace hearth. "It seems that your aunt was going to do some trimming on the window screens. She was carrying an open bucket of paint — a gallon bucket — when she saw a little garter snake."

"Snakes always have frightened her," Ellen said.

"This snake was no exception. Your aunt dropped the paint bucket, and it took Doug and me the rest of the day to clean up the mess. Even so, there are a million tiny stains that just wouldn't come up."

"So you're measuring my room today?"

"Right." Frank smiled. "Hope you don't mind. When I saw your room was empty, I seized the opportunity to begin measuring before you returned. I'm just about finished. I'll be out of your way soon."

Ellen closed her empty suitcase and set it in the closet. "Take your time. I wouldn't want to cause you to make any errors in the new heating-system plans." Ellen wandered back out into the hallway and studied the oil paintings on the walls and the Oriental carpets on the floors. Did Doug Cooper also live here on the second floor? He seemed agile enough. Aunt Madeleine must have put him up here somewhere. The doors that opened onto the central foyer were all closed, and she was afraid to open any of them lest someone think she was snooping. She had no idea which room was Frank's or which one might be Doug's. Frank had said his room was next to hers. But on which side? Or perhaps he hadn't been speaking literally. It could be any of the rooms near hers.

Presently Frank Welborn left her room and joined her in the hallway. "All finished. Your room measured just the same as all the others of its type. But I had to be sure. I like to be super thorough. A few inches can make a lot of difference when one is installing a new heating system."

"What sort of heating system does Scarlet Point have now?" Ellen asked, wishing she could edit all the "supers" from Frank's conversation.

"Just the fireplaces," Frank replied. "No doubt you've noticed them. One in each room. That's why the lodge has never been opened in the winter. Fireplace heat just won't do the job in Iowa's sub-zero temperatures. Originally the fireplaces were just intended to remove the chill from the rooms in the fall and spring or on an exceptionally cool summer evening."

"The hearthstones and mantels are picturesque," Ellen admitted. "But I had no idea that Aunt Madeleine intended to operate the lodge on a year-round basis. I wonder if that is really practical. Who would want to spend the winter here with nothing to do but stare out at the snow and ice?"

"Who knows?" Frank shrugged. "Maybe Spirit Lake will become a booming winter resort. But come with me for a minute and

I'll show you around up here. Your aunt's room is between mine and Doug's. She also has a room downstairs, and most of the time that's the one she uses. There are just four people on the second floor. Of course your aunt pictures every room full by the end of the summer, but that's a lot to ask for. There are forty-six rooms downstairs that are still unoccupied."

"Forty-six!" Ellen exclaimed. Rich as Aunt Madeleine was, Ellen wondered if she could really afford to open Scarlet Point Lodge to only four paying guests. Sentiment had surely impaired her sense of reason. Where were her advisors, her business manager?

Ellen followed Frank as he opened doors to empty rooms all up and down the corridor and around the rotunda that opened onto the floor below. Some of the rooms were furnished. Others were bare. Scarlet Point Lodge was a structure of mammoth proportions. The rooms were not large, but there were hundreds of them.

"Come on up to the third floor," Frank invited. "There's a super fireplace in one of the rooms up there that you'll be interested in."

Ellen followed Frank to the third floor, feeling the heat and inhaling a musty, closed odor. She wiped away perspiration that beaded on her upper lip, and she felt a bit dizzy when she peered over the chest-high railing that ringed the open rotunda. It was an effort to gaze down at the first floor far below, and she soon left the railing and followed Frank.

"Here it is," Frank said, flinging open a door. "Feast your eyes. The fireplace is made of native stone like all the others, but the mantelpiece has been carved from marble. Years ago it served as a countertop in a local drugstore, and before that the marble slab was part of a bathhouse in Italy — Florence."

Stepping inside the room, Ellen ran her fingers over cool marble the color of gray slate. As she examined it closely she could see fossils of tiny sea creatures embedded in the stone. The room was furnished in fine mahogany, but the fireplace dominated the scene.

"It's beautiful, Frank. It really is. This room must have belonged to someone very special."

"A duchess or a princess or some such. Your aunt told me about it. The woman came here each summer for years. She and your aunt were close friends."

Ellen walked across the floor to the window overlooking the lake, and as she did so her eye caught a bit of purple something on the floor near the bed. Stooping, she picked up a bow tied from a short length of purple yarn.

"What'd you find?" Frank asked.

"Just a piece of yarn, but —"

Ellen had been going to add "but it's wet" when the piercing scream interrupted her. Although they were three stories up, the scream seemed to come from outside the window. Ellen and Frank both rushed to look.

"What on earth!" Frank muttered.

As if on signal, the scream shrilled a second time. Unhooking the window screen, Ellen pushed it out and looked up. Far above her, Aunt Madeleine stood on the narrow railing of one of the many Spanish belfry towers that decorated the roof of the lodge.

"Frank! We've got to do something. She could fall any minute. How do you suppose she got up there?"

Frank took one quick look; then he sprinted from the room. "There's a construction crew down the road a piece," he shouted over his shoulder. "I'll see if they have ladders."

Ellen heard Frank running downstairs, but she dashed on up the next flight of steps.

The fourth floor was a warming oven, but Ellen hardly noticed. After trying three doors she rushed into the room directly under the belfry where her aunt was. Tugging at the window, she managed to open it and remove the screen. She leaned out, looking upward, shading her eyes from the sun's glare.

"Aunt Madeleine!" Ellen shouted. Then she lowered her voice. She mustn't alarm her aunt. "Aunt Madeleine, try to relax. Frank's gone for help. Everything's going to be all right. Men are coming with ladders. Construction workers. We'll have you down in no time."

Aunt Madeleine stopped screaming and looked down at Ellen. In her lavender jersey robe she looked like a ghost ready for a takeoff flight.

"Thank goodness you heard me, Ellen. I was afraid nobody could hear me, afraid nobody would miss me for hours and hours."

Ellen glanced down at the small cluster of guests who had gathered outside the lodge and who were craning their necks to see what was going on. One lady was peering at them through binoculars.

"Aunt Madeleine, can't you step down from that railing? Step down onto the floor of the belfry? It's really quite dangerous up there. If you lose your footing, you might fall."

"Drat it! Do you think I'm a complete idiot? Do you think I wouldn't step down if I could? I'm stuck up here. Or paralyzed with fright. I can't move."

"Try," Ellen begged.

"If I move I'll fall for sure. Do something, Ellen! Don't just stand there staring at me."

"Frank's gone for help. There's nothing I can do but keep you company." Ellen eyed her aunt. In the bright sunlight Aunt Madeleine's face looked chalky white. Her sooty mascara made her eyes stand out like two burnt holes in a sheet, and her Cupid's-bow mouth looked as if it had been painted on with poster paint. The lavender ruffles of her robe fluttered in the breeze blowing in from the lake, and Ellen could see that her aunt was wearing high-heeled slippers that could slide off the narrow railing at the least movement of her feet.

"Don't try to move, Aunt Madeleine," Ellen called. "Everything's going to be all right." Ellen had no more than finished speaking the words she didn't believe when she heard a construction truck lumbering onto the patio. Then Frank alighted from the passenger side of the truck cab and began shouting orders to two men who began maneuvering long aluminum ladders.

"Hang on, Mrs. Ferris," Frank called, cupping his hands at the sides of his mouth. "Help's on its way."

Ellen was torn between staying where she was close to her aunt or joining the crowd below. Reluctantly she decided to stay where she was. She kept up a steady stream of conversation to try to calm her aunt, all the while keeping one eye on the activity below.

"Where'd the truck come from?" Aunt Madeleine asked. "What are those men doing?"

"I think they're men from the construction site down the road a ways. At least that's what Frank said. They'll have you down from here in no time at all. They have experience in using those ladders. You can trust them."

"They make me feel like a stray cat," Aunt Madeleine complained. "That's what men with ladders do. They rescue stray cats from tall trees and telephone poles. I'm being humiliated right here on my own property."

"Hang on, Aunt Madeleine," Ellen said. "You're not being humiliated. Just concentrate on hanging on. The men are stretching a ladder up to you right now."

Ellen's mouth felt as dry as a new blotter

while she watched the men ease the ladder into place, watched Frank begin the long climb to the belfry while the two helpers held the ladder steady. She gasped. She had expected Frank to hold the ladder, expected the construction men to make the rescue.

"Don't touch me," Aunt Madeleine screamed when Frank neared her. "Don't touch me or I'll fall for sure. Keep away."

"Mrs. Ferris, I've got to touch you in order to get you down from here," Frank replied, keeping his voice calm and smooth. "Now, you just try to do what I say."

When Frank reached a level with Aunt Madeleine, he leaned from the ladder and put one arm around her waist. Ellen couldn't bear to watch. She turned her head, and the next time she dared look Aunt Madeleine was on the ladder climbing down. Frank was below her, giving her directions. She took a step every time Frank told her to take a step, and at last they both stood on the ground with her guests and the construction workers. Ellen ran down three flights of stairs to join them.

"How can I ever thank you?" Aunt Madeleine was asking Frank as Ellen joined the group. "I'm so embarrassed. I had no idea that —"

"It's all right, Mrs. Ferris," Frank said.

"And don't thank me. Thank these other men."

"We just did our duty," one man said. "You call on us again if you need us. Lucky we were in the vicinity. Lucky the ladders were long enough."

Ellen sensed that the men were glad to get away from the lodge, and she didn't blame them. She rushed to her aunt.

"Are you all right?"

"Of course I'm all right. I could have got down without any help if you had just given me time."

"I'm sure you could have," Ellen lied, "but we wanted to be on the safe side. You come on inside now and relax for a few minutes. I'll make us some coffee."

"I don't know about the desirability of this lodge," one man said to another.

For the first time Ellen considered the lodge guests, whom she hadn't yet met.

"Me either," the second man replied. "I think the old dame's loony. I think she's out of it. Imagine pulling such a trick as that."

As Ellen was trying to think of something to say to soothe the guests, a short, squat woman with snow-white hair caught under a silver net stepped forward. She had been watching the scene with the others, but now she took command.

"You people follow me and let Miss Madeleine catch her breath. If she was up on the belfry, she had good reason to be up there. You all come along now. I've coffee and hot cinnamon rolls just waiting to be buttered. Come along."

"Thank you, Josie," Aunt Madeleine said. "Thank you very much."

Ellen didn't know whether it was Josie's commanding voice or the scent of cinnamon rolls that persuaded the guests to follow her to the kitchen. Even Frank and Doug went with the group, leaving Ellen and her aunt alone on the patio.

Ellen settled her aunt in an easy chair in the huge parlor, then went to the kitchen for coffee. When she returned, Aunt Madeleine had a bit more color in her cheeks and she seemed calm and composed.

"I suppose you think I'm a fool," Aunt Madeleine said. "And I suppose I owe you an apology."

"I've tried not to draw any conclusions," Ellen said. "And no apologies are necessary. But suppose you explain just a wee bit. What were you doing up in the belfry? I won't even ask you how you got there. The why is more important."

"It sounds silly when I say it out loud," Aunt Madeleine admitted. "But I heard on

the early-morning news that the temperature was to soar into the nineties today. We
have no air conditioning as yet, so I went
up on the fourth floor to open some windows in hope of getting a cross breeze. Then
I saw this baby bird. A robin."

"In the lodge?" Ellen asked.

"No. It was on the edge of the belfry
squawking for its mother. I thought surely it
would fall, so I climbed through an attic
opening into the belfry to try to rescue it.
The bird hopped away from me. I stood on
the railing to try to reach it, and the darn
thing flew off. Guess it was old enough to
fly after all. Then I looked down to see
where it had gone. I should never have
looked down. I was okay as long as I was
looking straight ahead. But once I looked
down at the ground I was paralyzed. I was
like stone. I couldn't move. It was absolutely
awful. I suppose I'll be a laughingstock."

"I won't let anyone laugh at you," Ellen
promised. "You thought you were doing the
right thing. Sometimes it's hard to know
just what's right and what isn't. But Josie
has saved you, I think. Why don't we join
the others in the kitchen? I think a brief
apology will smooth things over."

Ellen led the way to the kitchen, feeling
embarrassed over the strange antics of her

aunt. But why should she be embarrassed? As she approached the kitchen she knew the answer. She didn't want to appear foolish in Frank Welborn's eyes. It was that simple.

CHAPTER FOUR

Ellen talked with her aunt until she calmed down, but when they reached the kitchen door, Aunt Madeleine held back.

"I should change clothes, Ellen. Being well dressed always gives me confidence. And if I ever needed confidence I need it now."

Ellen nodded. She accompanied Aunt Madeleine to her room and helped her change from her robe into morning clothes. When they came downstairs again, the lodge guests along with Frank and Doug were still seated at a large round table in the kitchen. Josie was serving breakfast. Conversation stopped as Aunt Madeleine and Ellen approached the table and sat down.

"I want to apologize for all the trouble I caused this morning," Aunt Madeleine said. "But nobody was hurt and no damage was done, so I suggest we forget all about it. Right now I want you to meet my niece,

Ellen Ferris, from the West Coast. Ellen will serve as nurse in our soon-to-be-established first-aid center."

To Ellen's surprise the guests responded to her aunt's introduction with polite applause. She smiled and nodded, but Aunt Madeleine wasn't finished.

"I understand you've already met Doug and Frank, Ellen, so I'll go on from there. The gentleman on your right is Judge Cloud. Retired, of course. Nothing the judge likes better than a good game of double solitaire."

Ellen hoped she could keep the guests sorted out in her mind and attach the right name to the right face. Judge Cloud would be easy. He was a rotund man with a cloud of white hair.

"And on the other side of Judge Cloud is Mrs. Young," Aunt Madeleine continued. "Mrs. Young is a former schoolteacher, so you two should have lots to talk about."

Ellen nodded at the plump, gray-haired lady. "I'm pleased to know you, Mrs. Young."

"Miss Speer is a retired secretary," Aunt Madeleine said, nodding toward the thin, reedlike woman across the table from her. "And she's a bird-watcher. Anything about birds you want to know, just ask Miss Speer."

Again Ellen smiled and acknowledged the introduction. Miss Speer was a wrenlike woman who perched on the edge of her chair and peered at Ellen from beneath feathery bangs. Ellen would have been unsurprised had Miss Speer chirped her greeting.

"Don't forget me — Mr. Boast."

Ellen turned to her left to smile at the man who had introduced himself in a voice like a bass viol. "How do you do, Mr. Boast."

Ellen noticed that while the rest of the guests were eating a hearty meal of eggs and cereal and toast, Mr. Boast was nibbling at a bowl of orange yogurt. Ellen remembered from her aunt's previous descriptions that Mr. Boast was the healthy one of the quartet. Perhps yogurt was the thing.

Once Aunt Madcleine completed the introductions everyone concentrated on eating. Josie hovered in the background, ready to pass seconds or pour coffee. Ellen noticed that Doug Cooper ate sparingly, while Frank Welborn took seconds on everything, including cereal.

Later the breakfast conversation touched on many subjects, from the mating habits of a yellow-bellied warbler to the plot development of the newest soap opera on TV. Everyone kindly refrained from mentioning Aunt Madeleine's unfortunate escapade on the belfry tower.

After breakfast Ellen lingered near the dining table until the guests went about their own pursuits. The parlor was large and cool, and Mrs. Young settled herself in front of the TV while Judge Cloud pulled a chair up to a small table and began dealing out a game of solitaire. Mr. Boast headed toward the lake for what Ellen guessed to be his morning walk, and Miss Speer picked up binoculars and settled herself in a yard chair on the spacious patio overlooking the lake.

"Whenever you're ready I'll show you the rooms I've chosen for your first-aid station," Aunt Madeleine said to Ellen. "They're nothing fancy, but they're large and well ventilated."

"Fine. But first I want to speak to Josie. She's a marvelous cook. Where did you ever find her?"

"I placed an ad for a cook in the local newspaper," Aunt Madeleine said. "Josie worked here years ago under different management, and I think she came back for old time's sake." Aunt Madeleine's charm bracelets jangled as she reached up to pat a blue curl into place. "I know I'm lucky.

Josie's a gem. All the guests rave about her cooking."

Ellen stacked a pile of dishes and carried them from the round table to the kitchen sink, thinking that Josie really needed a helper to assist with the menial chores.

"Josie, I want you to meet my niece, Ellen," Aunt Madeleine said.

Josie was scowling, but when she saw Ellen, her face brightened and she smiled.

"Good morning, miss. It's nice to have you with us for the summer. Did you have a good trip from the West Coast?"

"Yes. It was a long trip, but I enjoy driving. I want to tell you how much we appreciated your quick thinking this morning. If you hadn't had rolls and coffee at hand, our guests would have been quite disturbed by the little upset we had here."

Josie beamed, and her ruddy face flushed with pleasure. "Why, thank you, Miss Ellen. You're very kind to notice. To my way of thinking good food can distract almost anyone from unpleasantness."

Ellen was almost embarrassed to see how much her compliment had pleased the cook. An expression of gratitude was such a small thing, yet how much it could mean! Suddenly Ellen realized how dependent Aunt Madeleine was on Josie Beanblossom. The guests at Scarlet Point Lodge had little to think of except their own comfort, and somehow comfort and a full stomach can be synonymous.

"Let me help you clear the table," Ellen offered. "You've been on your feet for a long time this morning."

"That isn't necessary, Ellen," Aunt Madeleine said. "You have other more important duties."

"They can wait a few minutes." Ellen headed back to the table. Everything about Scarlet Point Lodge was big, and she knew it would take a lot of steps to carry all the breakfast things from table to sink.

"Here, Miss Ellen," Josie called after her. "If you want to help, use this cart. It saves time as well as steps."

At that moment Frank appeared and motioned to Aunt Madeleine, who joined him at a desk in the parlor. He had changed clothes, and now he wore apricot-colored slacks, shirt, and shoes. He and Aunt Madeleine were deep in conversation as Ellen continued to help Josie clear the breakfast table. As they passed in front of the door between the kitchen and the dining room, Ellen couldn't help noticing the dark glances Josie tossed in Frank's direction.

"Is something the matter between you and Frank?" Ellen asked, hoping Josie wouldn't think she was prying.

"That one!" Josie lifted her chin in an angry tilt. Then she relaxed. "I should say nothing, miss. Nothing at all. Mr. Frank Welborn is hired to work here just as I am. His doings are no concern of mine. As long as your aunt is happy with his services, that's all that matters."

"But something's wrong," Ellen said. "I can tell. Better let me in on it, Josie. If there's been a misunderstanding, perhaps I can help straighten it out without hurting anyone's feelings."

Josie let the swinging door between the kitchen and the dining room whoosh shut behind them before she spoke again. She began running water into the sink; then she looked up at Ellen, pausing with her dish-cloth in midair.

"Food has been disappearing from this kitchen, miss. At first I thought I was imagining it. I pride myself on providing ample meals. Nobody can say they have left Josie Beanblossom's table hungry. It sort of makes me boil to have someone sneaking food behind my back."

Ellen picked up a dish towel and began drying the dishes Josie washed. Didn't they have a dishwasher? she wondered. Was everything at the lodge antiquated and inadequate?

"Are you sure about the food disappearing?" Ellen asked. "Perhaps someone ate it and you just didn't happen to notice at the time."

Josie shook her head, and her face flushed again, this time in anger. "Someone's snitching. Like I said, yesterday it was small stuff I missed — half a loaf of bread, an orange, a handful of cookies."

"The food just started disappearing yesterday?" Ellen asked.

Josie nodded. "But this morning's different. A whole cherry pie has disappeared. Vanished. I got here early this morning — always do, as far as that goes. But this morning I was a bit earlier than usual, because I wanted to bake those pies for lunch before I started preparing breakfast. Three cherry pies, mind you — three pies I baked. And how many do you see there on the counter now? I ask you. How many?"

Ellen looked toward the counter. "Two. You're right, Josie. There are only two pies left."

"Someone snitched one of them during that flap with Miss Madeleine on the belfry tower and all. And I'm betting on Frank

Welborn. He's the one with the king-size appetite."

"But Frank was busy rescuing Aunt Madeleine."

"Can't help that," Josie said. "Frank Welborn thinks big, and he eats big. He's the only one who could wolf a whole pie all by himself. 'Twould give the others indigestion."

"Perhaps we should mention the loss to Aunt Madeleine," Ellen suggested.

Josie shook her head. "I don't want to do that. Your aunt has enough problems without being bothered with kitchen details. It would only upset her."

"I suppose you're right." Ellen picked up a dry cloth.

"I'll just keep a sharper eye out in the future," Josie said. "Josie Beanblossom's smarter than any food snitcher. It was just that this morning everybody was so excited and all. A thief could have sneaked in here and stolen the whole kitchen for all of me. I was out on the patio praying that Miss Madeleine wouldn't fall and break every bone in her body."

"I can understand that," Ellen said. "But you shouldn't have to keep constant vigil over your food. You let me know if anything else disappears."

Josie shrugged. "Guess it really doesn't matter. These guests pay a flat fee for staying here, and that fee includes their food. According to my way of thinking, they're entitled to all they want to eat. It's just my pride that gets ruffled. I do try to serve up ample meals."

Before Ellen could reply, Aunt Madeleine swooped through the doorway, filling the air around her with the scent of lavender. "Ellen, do come with me now. We must get busy and organize your first-aid center. We could have an emergency at any time, and I do want to be prepared."

Ellen laid down her dish towel and smiled at Josie. "I'll see you later, Josie. And thanks again for the delicious breakfast."

"You'll spoil her," Aunt Madeleine said when they were out of Josie's hearing. "And I didn't bring you here to spend your time in the kitchen."

"Sincere compliments for work well done never spoiled anyone," Ellen said. She didn't even like to think what would happen to Aunt Madeleine if Josie took it into her head to leave Scarlet Point Lodge.

Aunt Madeleine led the way through a wide archway to the left of the dining room. She stopped at the first door on that corridor and stood and gestured at a red cross someone had painted on the white wood.

"How do you like that, Ellen? Do you think I should hire someone to letter the words 'First Aid' below the red cross?"

Ellen smiled. "I don't think that'll be necessary. Everyone will know what the room is for."

"The suite," Aunt Madeleine corrected. "I've chosen this two-room suite for your headquarters. No use to be crowded when we have so much space available."

They stepped inside the suite, and Ellen smiled as she strolled through both rooms. "This'll be fine, Aunt Madeleine. I can keep supplies and emergency equipment stored in the back room and use this front room as sort of a reception area for patients."

"I'm glad you're pleased." Aunt Madeleine began tugging at a chair that was wedged behind a couch. "I didn't have too much of the right sort of furniture to work with, Ellen, but I did find these few things. You decide where you want them put and I'll call Doug to help with the moving."

Ellen studied the rooms and the furnishings at hand while her aunt went to summon Doug. When they returned, Ellen spoke.

"I think we should shove the supply cabinets and one cot into the back room for privacy's sake, don't you? We could use a chair or two back there also. In this front room I'd like to have my desk and chair, some easy chairs for patients, and maybe even another rollaway cot if you have one around here someplace."

"I think we can arrange that," Aunt Madeleine said. "Doug, you help Ellen move these things while I go back for another cot. I think I saw one up on the second floor."

"Arranging the rooms isn't all that much of a job," Ellen said when her aunt left. "If you'll just help me with the desk, I think I can do the rest."

"No trouble at all," Doug said.

Before they were half finished with the moving, Ellen was glad that Doug was there to help. The supply cabinets were heavier than she had thought they would be, and while the cot was lightweight, it was a tricky thing to maneuver through the narrow doorway. When Aunt Madeleine returned with another cot, which was folded into a compact canvas-bound bundle, Ellen let Doug assemble it.

"Aunt Madeleine, I really feel I should have a private telephone here in the station and an extension in my room upstairs. Would that be possible?"

"Surely," her aunt said. "I'll call the telephone company this morning. And of course you'll need supplies for the station. I've telephoned the hospital. They're going to rent us some spare oxygen equipment until we can buy our own. Why don't you make a tentative list of things you'll need? Do it right now, then you can drive into town and buy what you're able to find and order the rest. Okay? I don't want to rush you, but I do want to have this center available for use just as soon as possible."

"Fine." Ellen nodded and sat down at her new desk. She was pleased to find paper and pencils in the top drawer, and she began jotting down items of needed equipment.

"What about a wheelchair?" Ellen looked up, expecting to see her aunt, but only Doug was there, leaning against the doorjamb.

"Fine with me. Maybe you should order two. Then we can hold races on the shuffleboard court. Should add a certain light touch to the recreation hour."

"I'm serious," Ellen said. "I know no one needs a wheelchair at the moment, but one should be available in case of emergency. And they're expensive."

"Emergencies?"

"Wheelchairs."

"Maybe you could rent one temporarily," Doug said. "I know where the rent-all store is. If you're ready to go into town, why don't you let me take you? I have a large car, and you could haul stuff back in it easier than in your VW."

Ellen felt her face flush with pleasure, and she hoped Doug didn't notice. She felt attracted to this man. He saw things in this country that others didn't see. Doug looked beneath the surface of things, and Ellen found that an admirable quality. But she hadn't come to Iowa seeking a summer romance. One moment she had been fascinated by Frank, and now Doug had her flustered. What was wrong with her? She needed to keep her mind on her business — business both here and back at her hospital in California. But Doug was waiting for an answer.

"I'd appreciate a limousine and a tour guide, Doug. Are you ready to go?"

CHAPTER FIVE

Ellen took time to change into a white nurse's uniform before they started to town. She had learned that looking professional often paid great rewards. Doug whistled when she came down the stairs, and she stood a bit straighter. Somehow he had a knack for looking well dressed even in work pants and a T-shirt.

"I'll phone ahead and tell the hospital people you're on your way," Aunt Madeleine called as Ellen and Doug started to leave the lodge.

"Thanks." Ellen waved to her aunt, then followed Doug to the parking lot.

Ellen had thought that under a flood of bright sunlight Scarlet Point would seem less eerie than it had at midnight. But the lodge still had a closed, deserted look that cast a pall in spite of blooming beds of petunias, the robins singing full blast, and the half-grown rabbits playing in the tall grass.

"This place is creepy," Ellen said. "There's something about it that gives me the shivers."

Doug nodded and his gaze met Ellen's. "Sometimes I think the earth gives off vibrations to those who are tuned in to notice, to feel."

"You mean you think this area's haunted?"

Doug laughed. "No. I don't believe in ghosts. But I do believe there's a universal thought bank that's made up of every thought and every idea that has ever existed. And I believe that each individual mind is an inlet that's in some mysterious way connected to this huge thought bank. I know from experience that a thinking person can have a feeling for events that have happened in a particular place. Even if I'd never read a word about the Spirit Lake massacre, I know I would have sensed a feeling of death when I visited this area. It's all around us."

Ellen shuddered. Doug reminded her a lot of Big Spirit Lake — ever turbulent and uneasy. She tried to concentrate on the sunshine, the blue sky, and the cars full of tourists who had come to the lakes with nothing more serious on their minds than a fun vacation. She and Doug drove along in silence until they reached the village of

Spirit Lake.

"There's a neat museum here," Doug said. "It's in an old railroad depot. Dickinson County Museum. Some day when we have more time I'll take you to see it if you'd like to go. There's a map on one wall that shows the exact location of each cabin that Inkpaduta and his warriors burned."

Ellen sighed. "Doug, I'd like to forget about that massacre if you don't mind."

They drove on a bit farther; then Doug stopped the car in the hospital parking lot. "I'll wait here while you go inside, Ellen. Take your time. I've brought my clipboard, and I can write deathless prose while you transact your business."

"Thanks, Doug. I'll try not to be too long."

Inside the hospital Ellen sniffed the familiar medicinal odors that were usually a part of her life. Was there a nursing school here? she wondered. But why did she care? She was well established in her California school.

"I'm Ellen Ferris," Ellen said to the woman at the reception desk. "I believe my aunt, Madeleine Ferris, made an appointment for me with Mr. Coiner, the hospital business manager."

The woman smiled. "Yes. Mr. Coiner is

expecting you. Come with me."

Ellen followed the receptionist to a private office where Calvin Coiner sat behind a steel-gray desk. In fact, everything about the room was steel-gray — the carpet, the draperies, the furniture. And even Mr. Coiner had steel-gray hair and wore a steel-gray suit in spite of the warm summer day.

"Miss Ferris?" Mr. Coiner smiled as he stood and offered his hand. "The oxygen equipment I promised your aunt is ready for you to take with you. But it's heavy. Do you think you can manage it?"

"I have a friend outside in a car. He'll help with it. Aunt Madeleine and I appreciate your renting us this equipment, Mr. Coiner."

"We're always glad to cooperate," Mr. Coiner said. "Now, if you'll just sign these forms — a mere formality but a necessary one."

Ellen read through the forms quickly, signed her name, and returned Mr. Coiner's pen to him. "What pharmacy would you recommend for purchasing the other supplies I'll need? I'm familiar with none of them."

"Acme Drug is very good. Nice people to do business with. And they'll get quick results on anything they have to order for you."

"And what about rental services?" Ellen asked. "I'll need to rent a wheelchair and maybe some crutches."

"Barlon Rents-All is the place you're hunting," Mr. Coiner said. "You'll find whatever you need there, I believe. If not, give us another call and we'll see what we can do to help you out."

Ellen stood, and Mr. Coiner led the way from the room. He personally got the oxygen equipment for her — tanks, tubes, and regulators. Then he provided written instructions for its use. Putting everything onto a cart, he wheeled it outside and helped Doug load it into the trunk of his car.

"Thank you very much," Ellen said as they prepared to leave the parking lot. "I appreciate your help, and you'll be hearing from Aunt Madeleine."

"Pharmacy next?" Doug asked as they left the hospital and turned back onto the highway.

"Yes. Acme Drug. I have quite a long list of items to buy. Hope Aunt Madeleine's credit is as good as she seems to think it is."

"Her credit seems to be strong," Doug said. "There are those around here who say your aunt has more money than . . ." Doug stopped, embarrassed.

"Than common sense," Ellen finished. "I've heard the news before. Old stuff. But Aunt Madeleine means well. She wants to do the right thing."

Ellen was in the pharmacy for almost an hour while the attendant carefully assembled fever thermometers, blood-pressure gauges, bandages, antiseptics, and simple medications requiring no prescriptions. Doug came inside to help her carry her purchases out to the car.

"Now the rental store," Ellen said. "Then we'll be ready to go back to the lodge."

Doug drove to Barlon Rents-All. By this time the car trunk was full, so they had to load the folding wheelchair and the crutches into the back seat.

"Doug, I really appreciate your helping me with all of this equipment. Don't think I could have managed it alone."

"My pleasure, Ellen. But there's just one more thing. An important thing, too."

"What's that?" Ellen asked. "Do you have some errands to do while we're here in town?"

"Do you know what time it is?"

Ellen glanced at her watch. "One o'clock."

"Right. And my stomach is used to sustenance at least three times a day. How about having lunch in town before we go back to Scarlet Point?"

Ellen thought for a moment. "Maybe that would be a good idea. Josie will have the luncheon things all put away by the time we get back to the lodge. I hate to think of making extra work for her."

"Let's get sandwiches and colas to go," Doug suggested. "I'd like to show you a close-up view of the other two big lakes, and I'd like to drive you to the site of the Gardner cabin. There's a graveyard there and a monument. Members of the Gardner family were Inkpaduta's first victims."

Ellen grinned in spite of herself. "Okay. But let's eat at some pretty spot near the lake, and let's eat before we go to the Gardner cabin."

Doug stopped at a drive-in and picked up a quick lunch. Then they drove across a narrow isthmus where East Okoboji and West Okoboji almost joined.

"How about eating at that picnic table under the oaks?" Doug asked, nodding to his right. "We'll have a great view of West Okoboji."

"Fine. I'm hungrier than I realized."

Doug parked the car in the shade, and they spread their lunch out on napkins on the picnic table. A pine-scented breeze blew from across the lake, cooling them. "The Okobojis are calm and smooth," Ellen said. "Remember how rough Big Spirit was this morning?"

"You're thinking of the legend, aren't you?" Doug smiled. "In all fairness I should point out that Big Spirit has more surface for the wind to ruffle. Notice on a map sometime. Big Spirit's greater size could account for its seeming turbulence when the other two lakes are calm."

Ellen smiled. "I didn't ask for a logical explanation. Really, I prefer the legend."

As they ate their hamburgers Doug told Ellen more about the lakes, and his deep personal interest in the subject attracted Ellen until she felt involved also.

"West Okoboji is one of three 'blue' lakes in the world," Doug said. "Do you notice a difference in its color as compared with that of Big Spirit?"

Ellen glanced out over the water. "Now that you mention it, I do. Big Spirit seems more of a pewter color, and this lake really is blue. What are the other two 'blue' lakes? Is Lake Louise one of them?"

Doug nodded. "And Lake Lucerne. I've never seen the other two, but I like West Okoboji. The irregular shoreline gives a person a feeling of seclusion even though almost every foot of property along the lake-front is developed."

"I've noticed the beautiful beach homes," Ellen said.

"Maybe we can get together some afternoon and go for a swim. But when you're floating on an inner tube in a protected inlet, it's hard to imagine that you're surrounded by almost four thousand acres of water and thirty-two miles of beach."

Ellen glanced at her watch as they finished eating. "If we're going to the Gardner historical site, we'd better be on our way. Aunt Madeleine will start worrying if we're not home soon. She's eager to put her first-aid center into operation."

Doug tossed the debris from their lunch into a trash can, then helped Ellen back into the car. "The cabin isn't far from here."

They drove past an amusement park; then Doug began following arrows that pointed to the massacre site. As he parked the car under a linden tree in front of a private home, Ellen felt a sense of dismay and disappointment.

"What's the matter?" Doug asked. "Something bothering you? If the place upsets you, we can leave."

Ellen sighed and glanced at a small burial plot fenced with iron spikes, a small green that surrounded a tall monument, and a replica of the Gardner cabin. "I guess I was expecting something more elaborate. This street is hardly more than an alley, and people have built private homes almost on top of the Gardner graves."

"History is a crop that sometimes gets plowed under." Doug helped Ellen from the car, and they walked a few feet to view the Gardner family burial plot, the cabin, which was closed for repairs, and the tall monument. Ellen sniffed a faint odor of frying potatoes and onions and felt the sun pounding on her head and shoulders.

"What're you thinking?" Doug asked, breaking the silence between them.

"It's hard to put my thoughts into words without sounding like a real complainer. But this historical site is all so low-key. People fought and died here, yet this is all that's preserved. I expected more. Do you suppose people tend to underrate scenes close to home because they also tend to underrate themselves?"

"That's something to think about," Doug said, leading the way back to the car. "Most people do tend to underrate themselves. You're an astute observer of human nature. Ever thought of being a writer?"

"Never." Ellen smiled at the thought, and

at the same time she wondered why she couldn't solve her own problems if she were as astute as Doug thought.

When they were headed back toward Scarlet Point, Doug stopped at a drugstore. "Mind if I pick up an evening paper? Your aunt gets it at the lodge, but it's mailed there and the news is always a day late."

Ellen waited while Doug bought a paper. When he returned to the car, he pointed out an advertisement for a nearby summer theater. "Do you like to go to plays? I hear there are some excellent productions presented at this theater."

"Yes, I like drama." Ellen studied the ad, which listed the coming attractions at the theater. Then a small article under the entertainment ad caught her eye.

"Did you see this, Doug? There's a runaway child hiding in the vicinity of Spirit Lake — at least the authorities think that's where she is. She's been missing since the day before yesterday."

"Lots of runaways these days. Kids take off with a buddy and end up on the West Coast or in Colorado."

"But this is different. Really different. This runaway is a girl, and she's just twelve years old. She split from a J.B. Stone home, where she was supposed to live as a foster child while her mother serves a six-month jail sentence for shoplifting. How sad."

Doug swerved the car to avoid hitting a boy on a bicycle, and Ellen said no more as she read the rest of the article silently to herself. Suddenly she found herself holding her breath as she read how the girl was dressed: cut-off jeans, a purple shirt, one orange sock, and one purple sock — and her hair in a ponytail.

Remembering the purple yarn she had found on the third floor of the lodge that morning, Ellen almost mentioned it to Doug. Then she thought better of it. Her imagination was probably running away with her. Surely a twelve-year-old girl wouldn't be hiding out at Scarlet Point. Yet the yarn Ellen had found was the sort of yarn kids wear around their ponytails.

Her main reason for keeping quiet made Ellen feel guilty. Would she protect the girl should she find her hiding in the lodge? Ellen knew how it was to be a runaway. She could empathize and sympathize. After her parents had been killed in a car accident, she had run away from the first foster home the court had placed her in. She had hidden out in a public museum for almost a week, and she remembered how she had refused to talk to anyone until Aunt Madeleine and Uncle Brad returned from Europe and took her in temporarily in their New York apartment. The memory pained her even after all these years.

"Why so quiet?" Doug asked, turning his head to look at her.

Ellen shrugged. "Just thinking."

Doug grinned. "Good. I like people who think." He dropped his hand over hers where it lay on the car seat. Ellen made no move to pull away from Doug's touch. She forgot about the Spirit Lake massacre, runaway girls with ponytails, and deserted vacation lodges. For the present moment she was totally absorbed by Doug Cooper, author, handyman, and teller of legends.

CHAPTER SIX

Ellen and Doug arrived back at the lodge a little past midafternoon. All was quiet, and Ellen supposed that the guests were napping. She had hoped to be able to slip away and search some of the unoccupied third-floor rooms for signs of a runaway, but no such luck. Aunt Madeleine met them at the door, eager to see the first-aid equipment they had bought and rented.

Doug helped lug the oxygen equipment to the first-aid station. Then he and Ellen assembled the folding wheelchair and rolled it inside. Aunt Madeleine carried a pair of crutches, and she just missed knocking a lamp off the piano with the tip of one of them when Ellen came to her rescue.

After all the supplies had been carried to the first-aid center, Doug gave a mock salute. "If you don't mind, I'll be off now. I think Josie has a potato-peeling job waiting for me in the kitchen."

"Nonsense." Aunt Madeleine put her hand on Doug's arm. "Let Josie peel her own potatoes; she's hired to do the kitchen chores. You've spent enough time in lodge service for one day. Run on and write your novel. I know how it is. I know you writers need a lot of time to yourselves. The rest of the day is yours, Doug."

Aunt Madeleine made her announcement like a queen bestowing the crown jewels on a peasant. Ellen smiled in spite of herself, knowing all the while that Doug would peel the potatoes and file the experience under "Gathering Material."

Ellen let her aunt help store the supplies on the cabinet shelves. It was good for at least two people to know where things were. Tomorrow she would make an inventory sheet, listing the contents of each cabinet and each shelf.

"I've called the telephone company," Aunt Madeleine said. "A man will be here to install your telephone sometime tomorrow morning."

Ellen tossed an empty bandage carton into the trash. "Thank you, Aunt Madeleine. That's really quick service, and I appreciate it."

"Now, Ellen, I want you to set regular office hours here in this first-aid facility. I

75

didn't ask you here to operate a twenty-four-hour-a-day service, and I won't allow the guests to take advantage of you. I think if you open the door after breakfast — say around ten o'clock — and keep it open until around three in the afternoon, that should be sufficient. And of course you'll close it for an hour during lunchtime. What do you think of that plan?"

"It sounds good to me. Of course you'll have a key to the center won't you? We both should have keys. Then if anyone needs first-aid attention during off hours, they'll know where to come for it."

"I want you to have one day a week off," Aunt Madeleine said. "You can choose your day to suit yourself. And there's no reason it has to be the same day each week. Keep your schedule flexible. I really don't expect you'll be too busy here, but just having a nurse around will be a comfort to the guests. People tend to worry about their health when they reach a certain age."

"Of course," Ellen agreed. "Everyone should be concerned with health, no matter what their age."

Then, as if to contradict Aunt Madeleine's words, the guests began to drop in at the first-aid center. Aunt Madeleine smiled at Ellen and headed toward the kitchen.

"Good afternoon, Judge Cloud." Ellen smiled at the dignified gentleman and motioned him to a chair. "Is there something I can do for you before dinner?"

"Nothing special. Just came in to see what provisions you have here for old asthmatics like me. You have nebulizers? Oxygen?"

Ellen nodded. "Indeed we do. But you have your own medication with you, haven't you? I can't prescribe medicines, you know. Those have to come from your personal doctor."

Judge Cloud ran his fingers through his white hair. "I've got my own medication. Just wanted to be sure you had something extra in case I have a bad attack. I don't see a hospital bed."

"We don't have one," Ellen said.

"Sometimes I need to lie with my head elevated."

"I have a slant board and extra pillows," Ellen said. "And of course we're only minutes away from the hospital."

Judge Cloud rose and peeked into the back room. He thanked Ellen and wished her luck, then wandered back toward the TV in the parlor.

Judge Cloud had no more than left the first-aid center when Miss Speer entered, scowling and rubbing her left elbow.

"Guess I'm your first patient." Miss Speer showed Ellen her swollen arm. "Bumblebee big as a helicopter stung me. I was sitting on the lawn near a patch of clover glassing a baby blue jay in a pine tree when all of a sudden this striped bomber zoomed in on me."

Ellen examined the sting, which was angry red and swollen. "You seem to have removed the stinger, Miss Speer. Or perhaps the bee didn't leave one. Sometimes they don't." Ellen kept Miss Speer chatting about birds while she treated the sting. When the treatment was completed, she sent her on her way.

"Think you might as well prepare yourself to face the other two," Aunt Madeleine said, poking her head through the doorway of Ellen's office. "It's curiosity that's ailing 'em. Just pure curiosity."

Aunt Madeleine was right. Within the next five minutes Ellen was called upon to treat Mrs. Young for a slight headache and to give Mr. Boast a Band-Aid for his heel where his jogging shoes had rubbed a blister. Aunt Madeleine stepped back into the first-aid center after Mr. Boast left.

"At least they succeeded in making me feel needed." Ellen smiled at her aunt, then glanced at Mr. Boast's departing figure.

"Guess I'll close up for the day. Everyone has been here except Frank and Josie."

"You get some rest before dinner," Aunt Madeleine said. "I didn't expect you to begin your official duties until tomorrow. Josie rings a dinner bell. You won't miss hearing it. Nap if you can."

Ellen headed upstairs before someone else came along to demand her time and attention. She entered her room, knowing that Aunt Madeleine was listening and maybe watching. As soon as she sensed that nobody was around she slipped out into the hallway and took the stairs two at a time until she reached the third floor.

Feeling a bit foolish, Ellen peeked into the room where she had found the damp yarn earlier that morning. Had it been this same day? So many things had happened since sunrise that morning seemed a month ago. The room was empty except for a stripped bed and some meager furnishings. If anyone had been hiding there, they had covered all signs of it. Ellen sniffed. Did she smell cinnamon? She sniffed again. She must have imagined it.

Ellen tiptoed up and down the corridor opening and closing doors, peeking under beds, and poking into closets. There was room enough for a whole army to hide out on this third floor if they did it quietly enough. And what about the fourth floor? There must be over fifty rooms up there. She couldn't possibly search all of them before dinner. Perhaps she should let Doug in on her suspicions about the runaway. But no. She didn't want to do anything that would make her appear foolish in Doug's eyes.

Smiling, Ellen shook her head. This morning she had been worried about Frank's reaction to her, but now Doug's seemed much more important. At that moment Ellen heard Josie's dinner bell, so she hurried down to her room to comb her hair and change from her nurse's uniform into something fresh. She would forget about the purple yarn. Some cleaning woman had probably dropped it while making her rounds. But why had it been damp? And what cleaning lady would bother with unused third-floor rooms?

Ellen shoved the questions to a far corner of her mind and tried to forget them. She was no detective. She had come here as a nurse. Operating the first-aid center was her chief duty.

Frank winked at Ellen as they sat down at the table. Even as Josie began to serve the roast, Judge Cloud monopolized the dinner conversation with tales of some long-ago murder trial. Miss Speer yawned audibly while the others pretended polite interest. But Doug's interest was genuine. Ellen wondered if he would try to fictionalize the facts and use the story in some future novel he planned to write.

"After dinner we'll have shuffleboard on the east courts, where it's shady," Aunt Madeleine announced. "Everyone's welcome. Come one, come all. We should really organize some sort of tournament, don't you think? A competition might give the game a little spark."

"I'm for that," Mr. Boast said. "I'll organize us into teams and make a score chart. Losers can treat the winners at the end of the week."

"Treat them to what?" Miss Speer asked.

Mr. Boast shrugged. "We'll figure that out in due time. The first thing to do is get organized."

Ellen slipped into the kitchen while the guests gathered around Mr. Boast, each one offering suggestions for the good of the shuffleboard tourney.

"Josie, your roast was delicious," Ellen said. "And that vegetable casserole was out of this world. Do you ever give out recipes?"

"Why, of course, miss. I wouldn't think

you'd be doing much cooking, though."

"I really don't," Ellen admitted. "I usually eat at the hospital cafeteria. But if I have the recipe, I'll be prepared. Right?"

Doug whisked through the swinging door with a tray of glasses and coffee cups. "I'll wash tonight, Josie. You dry. Okay?"

Josie beamed. "You're a good boy, Doug. But why don't you and Miss Ellen go out for a walk? The lake's at its best this time of the evening. You two run on and I'll take care of the kitchen detail."

"Nothing doing," Ellen said. "We're here to help, and you can't talk us out of it."

Josie made no further protests, and Doug washed fast enough to keep up with both of them drying. Just as they were finishing their chore they saw Frank step out onto the back patio.

"My, doesn't he look nice tonight?" Josie said. "I'll hand that much to him. He really knows how to dress. Guess I have a weakness for handsome men in silk slacks and yellow sport coats. I rather envy the lady he's going to see tonight."

Ellen smiled, remembering Josie's anger at Frank that morning. Evidently she was not one to hold a grudge.

"How do you know he's going to see a lady?" Doug removed the sink stopper and let the dishwater gurgle down the drain.

"Why else would a fellow get all dandied up like that?" Josie asked. "I've learned that when men dress up there's usually a woman behind it somewhere."

Ellen laughed as she hung up her dish towel and told Josie good night. A few moments later Doug followed her out onto the patio overlooking Big Spirit. Frank had left and they were alone. The evening was soft and warm, and the scent of clover hung in the air.

"No yellow sport coat," Doug said. "No silk slacks. But if you'll come along with a character in jeans and a T-shirt, I'll row you out on the lake. Big Spirit is impressive at twilight."

"I'd love a boat ride."

"There's a catch," Doug added. "You have to help row."

"I'm used to that," Ellen said. "In California I sometimes spend a morning rowing a dinghy around a bay near my apartment. Where's your boat? And who owns it?"

"It's a flat-bottom rowboat and it's the property of the lodge, but your aunt has given me permission to use it whenever I please. Sometimes I take the men guests out for an afternoon of fishing."

Ellen followed Doug down the steps to

the quay; then they walked along the shore-line for several yards. Ellen watched while Doug pulled a weathered gray boat from a hidden spot under some willow limbs that dipped into the water. Easing the boat parallel with the shoreline, he motioned for Ellen to get in.

"Sit on the middle seat. We'll row together."

Ellen obeyed. Doug shoved them off; then he leaped into the boat, getting his feet only slightly wet.

"Where to?" Ellen asked.

"Let's head around that point on our right. There's a cove around there where we can get out and sit on a grassy bank and watch the moon rise."

They pulled the oars in perfect rhythm, and Ellen felt a oneness with Doug that she liked. He sensed when she needed to rest, and he eased up and rested with her. When they reached the cove, Doug guided the boat as close to the shore as he could. Then he leaped into the water and pulled the boat onto the bank so that Ellen could get out. "I'd hate to have to walk back," Ellen said. "We've come a long way."

"With you it might not seem so far." Doug smiled as he sat down on the grass, using a fallen elm for a backrest. Ellen joined him, and they sat listening to bullfrogs croak and watching purple shadows fall across the gray water. Now and then a muskrat etched a *V* in the water as it swam near the shoreline. Even in the still twilight Big Spirit looked choppy. Ellen noticed that the boat had a running light; it would be dark before they could get back to the lodge.

"Your aunt told me about some of your problems in California," Doug said. When Ellen looked at him in surprise, he added, "I'm sure she didn't mean to let out any secrets. But you know how she is, Ellen. She's genuinely concerned about you and your welfare."

"So much has happened today that I'd almost forgotten about California. Don't suppose you have any easy solution to my troubles."

"I'm sure that if there was an easy solution you would have discovered it."

"I haven't discovered anything at all. I'm just faced with a bunch of unpleasant choices. And I have to come up with some sort of decision in less than a week. If I let that girl continue nurse's training, if I compromise, I'm not sure I'll want to go on living with myself. And if I resign, I'm not certain I can live with that, either. I hate to have her expelled and do the hospital out of a large donation. What would you do?"

"It's a tough decision to make," Doug said. "What I'd do shouldn't influence you, though. The situation may give rise to one of those questions that has no completely satisfactory answer."

Ellen made herself more comfortable against the log. "It's a relief just to hear you say that, Doug. Everyone else, including Aunt Madeleine, has offered a pat solution, sure that theirs is the absolutely correct way of dealing with the situation. I thought for a while that I was the only person in the world who was unsure of exactly what was right." Ellen laughed. "It's a relief to know there are two of us."

Sitting quietly on the lakeshore with Doug helped Ellen to relax, yet she sensed that Doug was never completely relaxed. There was an unrest about him that troubled her, interested her. She had never known a man like Doug before.

The moon rose from the water like a platinum disk and glowed in the slate-colored sky like a medallion hanging from a chain of stars. Crickets chirped. Frogs croaked. Now and then a night bird loosed an eerie call to its mate. Presently Doug rose without speaking, helped Ellen to her feet, and motioned her into the boat.

They rowed back to Scarlet Point to the accompaniment of waves slapping against the sides of the boat. Doug let Ellen out on the cement quay, then eased the boat into its hidden spot beneath the willow branches. Ellen wished she could stop time and hold this peaceful moment forever.

Doug took her hand as they walked up the steps to the lodge. When they reached the patio, he pulled her into the shadow of a spruce, drew her close to him, and kissed her. Ellen's warm response to his kiss surprised her. She pulled away and hurried upstairs to her room.

What was she doing? She didn't want to fall in love with Doug Cooper or anyone else. She had enough entanglements in her life right now, and she wanted to handle them, to unravel them, on her own. It would be cowardly to fall in love and use marriage as an excuse for resigning from her job and her unsolved problems.

When Ellen fell into bed she was in a state of near exhaustion, yet she couldn't fall asleep. The warmth of Doug's kiss lingered in her memory. The mind's eye vision of Aunt Madeleine clinging to the belfry tower disturbed her. And suddenly she thought again of the bit of purple yarn she had found that morning.

She tried to sit up in bed, but she was too tired. She had searched the third-floor rooms once. A more thorough search would have to wait until tomorrow. If a child was hiding out at the lodge, at least she was in a safe place. But somehow Ellen didn't feel safe herself. She forced herself from the bed and padded across the floor to lock her bedroom door. Then she crawled back into bed.

CHAPTER SEVEN

Ellen overslept the next morning. When she looked at her watch it was almost eight-thirty. She barely had time to slip into her uniform and get downstairs for breakfast. There was no time to recheck the rooms on the third floor. What good would her searching do? Any child who was cunning enough to hide in the unoccupied portion of the lodge would be clever enough to change rooms every day. Tracking down such a person would be a difficult task.

The guests were milling about in the huge parlor when Ellen arrived downstairs. For the first time she noticed that the day looked gray and stormy. Big Spirit was frothed with whitecaps. She could hear a sharp wind blowing outside, could see it ruffling the leaves of the pin oak and lashing the supple willow branches.

"Good morning, Ellen," Aunt Madeleine called. "I was beginning to wonder about you. Looks as if we're in for a bit of a blow. But I always like stormy summer days. Your uncle Brad and I used to sit in this very parlor by a glowing fireplace and listen to symphonies on such days. I preferred Strauss waltzes, but I always let Brad choose the records. He liked Beethoven and Mozart."

"I can always predict a storm." Miss Speer looked down her nose with a superior air. "I can predict it by the bird activity — or non-activity, I should say." Miss Speer motioned toward the window. "Notice how you see no birds in flight right now?"

Mr. Boast nodded. "I'll be your straight man. Why don't we see any birds in flight?"

"Because atmospheric pressures before a storm make the air damp and heavy," Miss Speer explained. "It's hard for birds to fly under such conditions, so before a storm one usually sees many feathered creatures perched on utility wires, tree limbs, and such. I can always predict a storm, and I say we're going to have a big one soon."

"Humph!" Mr. Boast snorted. "I think it's a great deal easier and a lot more sensible to spot a storm just by looking at the sky. Or listening to the weather warnings on radio or TV. Those black clouds aren't fooling around. They're going to open up on us after a while."

Miss Speer flounced to the window overlooking Big Spirit and peered through her binoculars, which she wore around her neck. Presently she turned to the group.

"There's a beautiful pair of goldfinches perched in the weeping willow down by the shore. Anyone care for a look?" She removed the binoculars from around her neck and offered them to the group.

When nobody showed any special enthusiasm, Ellen stepped foward with a smile. "I'd like to see the finches, Miss Speer."

Ellen focused the binoculars and scanned the swaying willow branches. "I see them. I really do." Ellen looked at Miss Speer, then put the glasses back to her eyes. "These binoculars make me feel as if I could reach out and touch them." The finches hopped to a lower branch, and as Ellen tried to follow them with the glasses she saw the boat she and Doug had used the evening before.

Handing the binoculars back to Miss Speer and thanking her, Ellen then looked at her aunt. "Has someone been out boating this morning?"

"Of course not," Aunt Madeleine said. "Nobody goes out before breakfast. Not that it's a rule or anything. Everyone just prefers to eat before starting the morning's activities. Why do you ask?"

"Because the rowboat has been turned upside down and pulled up onto the shore under that willow. After Doug and I used the boat last night, we left it floating in the water. And right side up, of course."

"So you were out boating with Doug," Aunt Madeleine said. "How nice."

Ellen felt herself flushing as all eyes seemed to be gazing directly at her. Judge Cloud and Mr. Boast smiled, and Mrs. Young and Miss Speer nodded their heads approvingly.

"But aren't you concerned about the boat?" Ellen asked. "It would be too bad if anything happened to it."

"Don't worry," Aunt Madeleine said. "Someone passing by may have thought it was going to drift off and may have hauled it in as a favor to me. As long as the boat's still there I won't worry about it."

Josie announced breakfast by ringing the dinner bell, although everyone, including Frank and Doug, was waiting in the parlor by this time. The breakfast conversation centered on the weather. All the oldsters recalled the worst storms they could remember and described them in depth. Ellen listened with interest as she ate. Doug said little and ate little, but Frank devoured great quantities of pancakes and sausages in addition to a generous bowl of cooked cereal. Ellen wondered if any more food had disappeared from Josie's kitchen. She doubted that Frank was the culprit.

As the meal ended the lights flickered and grew dim. Aunt Madeleine hurried to find candles in case they needed them. Ellen dashed upstairs to brush her teeth. Then she returned to her first-aid station, unlocked the door, and sat down at her desk. She was just beginning to make an inventory list of the supplies she had purchased when Frank appeared in the doorway. As usual he looked like a fashion plate. This morning he wore an ocelot-print shirt over tawny slacks. A silk ascot matched his blond hair.

"Good morning." Ellen stood and smiled. "Is there something I can do for you?" She was glad she had decided to dress in uniform while on duty. Her white pantsuit and cap gave her a sense of confidence and dignity that she needed to stand up to Frank's penetrating gaze.

"Luckily my call is strictly nonprofessional, Ellen. I'd like to take you out to dinner tonight. There's this restaurant on West Okoboji called the Beachcomber. The cuisine is super, and the floor show is top-notch. How about it? Will you join me there this evening?"

"I'd love to go," Ellen said, sincerely pleased at the invitation. "What time should I be ready?"

"If we leave here around seven, we'll get there in time for most of the dinner dance music before the first floor show. How does that sound to you?"

"Fine. I'll be ready."

"Good deal. I'll meet you in the parlor." Frank laughed. "Guess we won't have any trouble finding each other."

Frank left the first-aid station, and Ellen waited until the sound of his footsteps had died away before she stepped into the hallway. She was heading to the kitchen to tell Josie that she and Frank wouldn't be eating dinner at the lodge when the storm broke with full force. The lights went out, and gloom filled the lodge in spite of Aunt Madeleine's candles. Lightning flashed, and thunder rattled the windows.

"Mercy on us!" Miss Speer cried. "Is it a tornado? If it's a tornado we should go lie in a ditch."

"Everybody keep calm," Judge Cloud ordered in his deep courtroom voice. "I've been listening to my transistor. There are no tornado warnings, just severe thunderstorms. Don't panic. And no need to go running for the ditch just yet. By the way, Miss Speer, what ditch do you have in mind? I haven't seen any ditch around here."

"Don't stand in front of the windows," Aunt Madeleine said, allowing Miss Speer no time to reply. "That's what Brad used to say to me during a storm. He used to say, 'Madeleine, don't stand in front of the window.'"

"Why don't we all sit down in the center of the room?" Ellen suggested, trying to calm the guests. "Perhaps we could listen to records."

"Electricity's off," Mrs. Young said. "No lights. No records. No TV. I'm missing my favorite morning program."

"Maybe we could tune in some music on Judge Cloud's transistor," Ellen said. "Music would be pleasant listening, and we'd be informed of any threatening conditions."

"Where's Mr. Boast?" Miss Speer's shrill voice rose like a siren, silencing the others. "I saw him go outside right after we ate. He always goes for a morning stroll. He's not here. I don't think I saw him come back inside."

"He always goes out to do deep-breathing exercises every morning," Judge Cloud said.

"Think he'd know better on a day like this."

"I'll go look for him," Doug volunteered. "He may be in some sort of trouble."

"Wait." Aunt Madeleine rushed to a closet. "Here. Wear my raincoat. You'll get soaked without a wrap."

To Ellen's surprise Doug slipped into the lavender coat with all its buttons and bows without protest. Then he ducked his head and stepped into the storm. The smell of rain and the feel of cold air rushed through the open door before Doug could close it.

Outside, the willow trees bowed to touch the ground. As the wind screamed under the eaves Ellen expected to see trees uprooted at any minute. But the sturdy oak beside the steps leading to the water stood straight and tall. Maybe the storm wasn't so bad after all. Maybe it was diminishing, Ellen thought.

Ignoring Aunt Madeleine's advice to stay away from the windows, Ellen pressed her nose against the cold glass, searching for a glimpse of Doug. Where was Frank? Why didn't he go help Doug search for Mr. Boast?

"I see them, miss." Josie came running from the kitchen, wiping her hands on her apron. "Mr. Doug has found the old gentleman, and they're heading back for the lodge. Wind's against them, though. They'll have a real struggle."

Ellen peered into the storm until her eyes watered, and at last she saw the flash of her aunt's lavender coat. Doug had linked his arm through Mr. Boast's arm, and they were leaning into the wind as they struggled toward safety. Ellen had her hand on the doorknob, ready to open the door for them, when a sound like a shot silenced everyone.

Then Ellen saw the oak tree sway and start to fall. Flinging the door open, she screamed to warn Doug and Mr. Boast, but the tree crashed to the ground, drowning out her voice. Ellen ducked back inside the lodge barely in time to avoid being hit by the branches. Glass shattered. A cold, damp wind licked through the broken window. Then all was quiet. Even the storm let up, as if satisfied that its fury had done all the damage it could for the present moment.

Aunt Madeleine was sobbing quietly, unmindful that her mascara was running down her cheeks. Miss Speer tried to soothe her. Ellen dashed outside and picked her way over the oak branches. The tree had split about twenty feet up, and half of it had come crashing down. But Ellen's concern was not for the tree. Where was Doug? Where was Mr. Boast?

"Doug? Doug, are you all right? Mr. Boast? Where are you?"

Oak branches rustled, and Doug scrambled to his feet. Ellen ran to him, relieved to see that he was unhurt except for a few scratches. Together they helped Mr. Boast to his feet. Blood streamed from his nose and from a gash on his head, and one sleeve was ripped from his shirt. With Doug on one side and Ellen on the other they helped Mr. Boast into the lodge and straight to the first-aid center.

"Lie down on the cot, Mr. Boast," Ellen said. "Try to relax. I'll give you a sedative and you'll soon feel better."

"No reason to lie down," Mr. Boast said, sitting on the chair beside Ellen's desk. He patted at his nose with a handkerchief. "I'm no invalid. I may be seventy-seven years old, but I'm in perfect health."

"But you've had a severe shock, Mr. Boast," Ellen said. "Please humor me just this once. I really think you should lie down for a few minutes."

"And I think I shouldn't." Mr. Boast jutted his chin toward the ceiling, ignoring the blood that was still running down the side of his face.

Ellen didn't argue. She brought a blanket from the cot and wrapped it around Mr.

Boast's shoulders, then filled a wash basin with warm water. Taking a clean cloth, she began to wash his cuts and scrapes. The worst wound was on his head, and it was some moments before Ellen could get the bleeding stopped, but at last she succeeded. Then came antiseptic and bandages. Soon Mr. Boast was feeling better.

"Would you like to go to your room?" Ellen asked. "Maybe you'd be more comfortable lying down there."

"Yes. That would be fine. I need a clean shirt and dry pants. And perhaps I will lie down. Just for a few moments, of course. I thank you for your kind attention."

Ellen smiled at Mr. Boast's grit, and although she walked with him to his room, she made no pretense of trying to help him. The other guests surged forward as Mr. Boast emerged from the first-aid center, but Ellen motioned them back. Mr. Boast walked with dignity, looking neither to right nor left. Ellen left him at his door and returned to the others.

By now the sun was shining again, and a double rainbow arched across the sky. Ellen felt as if she could use a good-luck omen.

"How is he?" Aunt Madeleine asked. "Should we call a doctor or take him to the hospital?"

"He'll be all right," Ellen said. "Just a few cuts and scrapes. He's not one to baby himself. But what about Doug? Was he hurt?"

"Does it look like it?" Aunt Madeleine nodded toward the fallen tree. Ellen looked and saw Doug already working hard at cleaning up the mess. Judge Cloud had joined him, and together they were dragging branches from the patio and stacking them out of the way on the lawn. Even Miss Speer was outside with a broom, trying to sweep up some of the mess.

"I've called a tree-trimming service," Aunt Madeleine said. "They'll be out in due time. I guess there're oaks down all over town. I didn't realize that such stout-looking trees were so brittle."

Doug came to the first-aid center later in the morning, and Ellen treated his cuts and scrapes.

"You were lucky," Ellen said. "That tree could have killed you."

"I saw it coming," Doug said. "I think Mr. Boast would have walked right into it if I hadn't jerked him back. Then he saw it, too, and we ran as hard as we could. Good thing he's in shape. His jogging paid off in a big way. I'll never laugh at anyone's health regime after that close call."

"He's a proud man," Ellen said, "and a stubborn patient. But I can't help admiring him."

Doug started to leave the center; then he turned. "By the way, the museum is open tonight. Would you like to go take a look?"

"I'd love to, Doug. I really would, but I've made other plans for this evening. May I take a rain check on the invitation?"

"Sure thing. The museum'll still be there tomorrow." Doug smiled at her. "Have you reached any decision yet about that California situation?"

Ellen shook her head. "None. It's hard to keep my mind on Janey Van Allen and the hospital board when there's so much going on around here."

At noon everyone appeared at the luncheon table, including Mr. Boast, and Josie smiled her pleasure as she received many compliments on her salad and sandwiches. After lunch Ellen rolled bandages in her office until closing time, when she locked the door and went to her room. Stretching out across the bed, she warned herself not to sleep, but the next time she opened her eyes it was almost six o'clock.

Ellen jumped up. Would she have time to shampoo her hair and dry it? She had to. She wanted to look her best for Frank; she knew he would expect it. Grabbing her shampoo, she hurried to the bathroom and enjoyed a combination shower and hair-wash. Then, back in her room, she tried to decide what to wear as she dried her hair with an electric comb.

The tailored shift? The long tailored skirt? Which would Frank prefer? Remembering that Frank seemed to like blue, Ellen decided on the long skirt. Pairing it with a sky-blue blouse, she was soon dressed and ready to go.

As she walked down the graceful stairway Ellen imagined herself at a great ball with a string orchestra playing and hundreds of guests dancing. Butlers served champagne in stemmed crystal, and maids offered dainty sandwiches on silver platters. That was the sort of thing that should be going on in a lodge such as Scarlet Point. Would Aunt Madeleine ever get this place on its feet again?

Frank was waiting for her by the front entry, and Ellen was conscious of his admiring gaze. She returned it with a pleased glance of her own. She had guessed correctly about what to wear. Frank wore white slacks and a blue sport coat. The fabric in his shoes matched the fabric in his blue and white print shirt. Ellen knew they made a handsome-looking couple, and she enjoyed the knowledge.

"Going out?" Aunt Madeleine asked, her charm bracelets jangling as she swooped down on them from the back of the room.

"Yes, Aunt Madeleine. Frank's taking me out to dinner tonight. I've told Josie not to count on us."

"Do have a good time, children. I've almost forgotten what it's like to go out in the evening."

"Why, Aunt Madeleine!" Ellen ignored her aunt's bid for sympathy and looked at her hand. "You've cut a finger. How did that happen?"

Aunt Madeleine hid her hand behind her back. "It's nothing, Ellen. Nothing at all. Just a scratch. I was just trying to remove a sliver of glass from the window where the tree broke it. Somehow it slipped, and before I knew it . . ."

"Come on in to the first-aid center and let me treat your finger properly," Ellen insisted. "You'll have an infection if you're not careful."

Frank scowled and sat down to wait. Ellen ran back upstairs for the key to the first-aid office. When she had her aunt settled on a chair near her desk, she went to work on her finger. The cut was deep and ugly looking, and Ellen spent several moments cleaning it out and applying a bandage.

"There you go," Ellen said when she finished. "Better come in and let me check on it tomorrow."

"Thank you so much, Ellen. It's good to have a nurse on the premises. Never thought I'd be the one to need your services, though." Aunt Madeleine walked to the front door with Ellen and Frank and told them good-bye. This time they were off.

"She's totally inept, Frank," Ellen said when they were in his car and on the highway. "Aunt Madeleine, I mean. That lodge is too much for her. She means well, but she's a social butterfly not a businesswoman. She needs someone to protect her from herself."

"That's why she called on you, isn't it?" Frank asked. "And I'm glad she did. Scarlet Point needed something to liven it up." Frank put his arm around Ellen and drove along slowly, seemingly unaware that they were going to be late to claim their dinner reservation. Ellen fought a nagging worry. She wondered if Frank was the type to make a scene if his reservation had been given to someone else. Ellen had lived through enough scenes for one day.

CHAPTER EIGHT

As they entered the village of Spirit Lake Frank put both hands on the steering wheel. He kept up a steady flow of conversation as they drove along.

"This area is one of the most popular vacation spots in Iowa, Ellen. But I suppose you already know that. A person can tell just by looking. I don't think there's an inch of undeveloped land on West Okoboji. Why, building lots that used to sell for eight or nine thousand are selling for many times that amount today. Real estate is big here. Big."

"It's a pretty area," Ellen said. "I don't know when I've ever seen so many oak trees."

"Some of the lake homes are in the hundred-thousand-dollar bracket, and the motels and inns are out of this world. They're making a mint for their owners. Every room is booked solid for the whole summer. That's why I'm staying at Scarlet Point. No place for me anywhere else. But I'm glad. For a while I thought I'd crawl up the walls from hearing Mr. Boast go on and on about his exercise and diet schedule and his past triumphs in the business world. And I thought I might fly if I heard another word from Miss Speer about her bird friends. And that Mrs. Young. Know what she does all day long?"

"What?"

"She watches soap operas on TV. But all that aside, your aunt is sitting on a gold mine out there. If that place were fixed up and managed properly, a person could make his fortune ten times over."

"Frank, have you ever thought of staying on at Scarlet Point? You have the know-how. As an architect you know what should be done to the place. Maybe you could work out some sort of partnership with Aunt Madeleine, a partnership that would work to the best advantage for both of you. Aunt Madeleine would be great as a hostess in an elegant lodge. She's like a steering wheel; she controls a lot of power, but she needs a firm hand to guide her."

"Nothing doing." Frank stopped at a traffic signal. "Roth and Roth, Incorporated sent me to Scarlet Point to redesign the heating system and to make plans for installing an elevator. That's as far as I'm concerned with the place. I've no money to invest just yet, and I wouldn't consider putting time and work into a lodge that I didn't own a piece of. Just doesn't make sense."

"What are you going to do when you've finished your project for Aunt Madeleine?"

"I'm going to the big time. New York. I'm only marking time with Roth and Roth. I'll never be content to settle down in some little town and watch my life go by. But every beginning architect needs experience. A super recommendation from Roth and Roth will mean a lot to me in New York. There's where the smart money is, New York."

As they drove past the amusement park Ellen had noticed the afternoon before when she was with Doug, a boy stepped onto the highway thumbing a ride. Frank swore under his breath and swerved the car to keep from hitting him. Ellen felt a muscle in her stomach tighten like a drawstring.

"I never pick up hitchhikers," Frank said. "Dangerous business. Only a super dope would trust a stranger in his car."

Ellen relaxed. As they passed the turnoff leading to the Gardner cabin and the historical monument she asked, "Have you visited the massacre site?"

"What massacre?" Frank looked down at her to see if she was joking.

"Oh, it happened years ago," Ellen said. "There's a restored cabin and —"

"Never cared much for local history," Frank said. "The past is past. I try to look to the future. This area as a whole does impress me. It's a vast enterprise. Just imagine the great wealth that's gone into developing this natural setting to resort proportions." Frank was silent for a few moments. Then he turned the car onto a lane leading to the Beachcomber, which overlooked a sparkling inlet on West Okoboji Lake.

"Here we are, and I'm starving." Frank parked the car in a crowded lot, then came around to open the door for Ellen. He took her hand, and they strolled toward the restaurant.

The rough-hewn logs of the exterior gave the building a rustic appearance, but inside the lobby the decor was ultramodern. As her heels clicked against the marble floor Ellen saw their reflection in a mirrored wall. Soft music and the fragrance of roses drifted from somewhere above them. Frank gave his name to a hostess, who returned his smile and removed the red velvet rope from across a stairway to their right.

"Go right on upstairs, Mr. Welborn. We've been expecting you."

Ellen sighed, relieved that the management had held their reservation for them. At the top of the stairway a host in a dark suit showed them to their table for two, which was right in front of the bandstand. The musicians had not started to play yet; the music Ellen had heard downstairs had been coming over a public-address system.

Ellen felt her shoes sink into the deep pile of the purple carpeting as the host held her satin-padded chair for her. All around them the other diners were deeply engrossed in their meals, and a hum of muted conversation filled the room. Once she and Frank were alone at their table Ellen spoke.

"This is a lovely place, Frank. I'm glad you thought of coming here. And this dining room is decorated in my favorite colors." She touched the lime-green tablecloth and glanced at the lemon-yellow sheers that had been drawn back from a glass wall so the patrons would have an unobstructed view of the lake.

"Wait until you hear the band," Frank said. "They're really the most. The lead trumpet man doubles on trombone, melophonium, and flugel-horn. The drummer writes their charts."

The fact that Frank must come here often impressed Ellen, but she forgot about it as the waiter presented menus in the form of leather-bound books some eight pages long.

"What would you like?" Frank didn't open his menu. "Seafood is the specialty of the house."

Ellen peered at her menu, only to find that many of the listings were in French. "I love shrimp," she said. "French fried."

"Fine." Frank looked at the waiter. "Make it two shrimp dinners. Tossed salads with oil and vinegar, baked potatoes with sour cream. Oh, and a bottle of wine."

"Your regular vintage, sir?"

Frank nodded.

At that moment the bandleader approached the bandstand. His red jacket, plaid vest, and white dress shirt topped dark slacks and well-polished shoes.

"He's going to unlock their horns," Frank said as the leader stepped onto the bandstand and pulled a key from his pocket.

For the first time Ellen noticed a thin red cable that stretched around all the band instruments. The cable was welded onto a support pole at one side of the bandstand, and it ran under the strings of the guitars and banjos, through the slide loops of the brass instruments, and beneath specially made fittings on the saxophones and clarinets. Although there were only five players in the group, Ellen counted thirty instruments. When the bandleader had unlocked and removed the protecting cable, the other four musicians joined him and began tuning their instruments.

"We have great seats," Ellen said. "We won't miss a thing. This is really super." She smiled inwardly as she heard herself borrowing Frank's favorite word.

The band began to play just as the waiter served their salads and hot bread. "Shall we eat or dance?" Frank asked.

"You said you were starved," Ellen said. "Why don't we eat our salads, then dance? Okay?"

"I was hoping that's what you'd say." Frank grinned at her and passed the salad dressing. "I knew you'd have a knack for saying the right thing at the right time."

Ellen laughed. "I just wish that were true."

"But it is," Frank insisted. "You have a talent for insight and empathy."

All at once Ellen found herself telling Frank about her problems with Janey Van Allen and the hospital board. She could tell by the way Frank listened that Aunt Madeleine hadn't given him a preview of the situation. "If I always said the right thing at the right time, I would have said it long ago and settled this business once and for all."

"I can't see that it's so difficult a decision to make." Frank added salt to his salad. "I'd just chuck the whole thing. That's what you should do. Bow out. Let the Van Allen girl continue her schooling. What do you care? Let some other teacher cope with her. The hospital will have its money. In due time the world will have another nurse. And in the meantime you'll have a better job somewhere else. That's the big thing."

"I wish it were that simple for me to figure out," Ellen said. "But I happen to believe that one girl's attitude toward her education is important. My stand on this matter could influence that girl's life. That's an awesome thought. I want to do the right thing — the right thing for everyone involved."

"You're really dead serious about that nursing school, aren't you?" Frank stopped with his fork in midair, looking at Ellen, staring at her as if he couldn't believe such a thing.

"Of course I'm interested in it," Ellen said. "I'm involved. It's a vital part of my life. I trained for years to qualify to teach. I hate to give up my job. I like that hospital, and I like that town."

"Is your hospital in a big city?"

"Mission Valley. A very small town. But the size of the town isn't important. Our hospital facility serves a large area. Bean farmers. Orange growers. Cattlemen."

"Why don't you go to New York? That's where things are happening. You aren't afraid to try making it in a big city, are you?"

Ellen took a sip of water, then continued eating her salad.

"Listen." Frank laid down his fork. " 'Misty.' The band leader knows that's one of my favorite tunes. How about dancing a few numbers?"

Ellen nodded, glad to end their uncomfortable conversation. They threaded their way through the dining tables to a small dance floor that overlooked the lake. The lights were low, and outside the moon lighted the cove. Three sailboats and an excursion boat were moored at a large dock, and here and there along the shore couples strolled arm in arm through the soft evening.

Frank was an excellent dancer, and Ellen felt at ease in his arms. Everything about him was vital, alert. He executed intricate steps with ease, and she followed his lead without faltering. In Frank's arms she forgot all about her troubles in California and her worries about her aunt. Frank was a man a girl could build a dream around.

"Guess we'd better get back to our table before our dinner gets cold," Frank said when the musicians ended a set of tunes. Ellen led the way from the dance floor. A waiter stood by a serving cart near their table, and when they were seated he set their shrimp dinners before them.

"Be sure to try their special tartar sauce," Frank said. "It's really special. Super."

Ellen ate her shrimp, thinking that she had never tasted anything so delicious in all her life. She and Frank didn't dance again. In fact they hardly visited as they ate. And when the waiter removed their plates, the musicians were leaving the bandstand.

"Please don't go away, folks," the bandleader said, speaking into a microphone. "That was just our dinner dance music. We'll be back in twenty minutes with the first floor show of the evening. Stick around."

Frank ordered orange sherbet, and they ate it while they waited for the band to return. Pulling his chair closer to Ellen's, Frank held her hand as the musicians returned and presented an hour-long floor show, hardly taking a break between tunes.

Each man played a variety of instruments, and all were featured on vocal solos as well as instrumental solos before the show ended.

On the drive home Ellen said, "I don't know when I've enjoyed an evening so much, Frank. It was a real treat. Perfect from beginning to end."

"The pleasure was all mine. Would you like to go out again tomorrow afternoon? There are lots of things to do around the lakes."

"I'd love to, Frank, but I have to man the first-aid station. I can't ask Aunt Madeleine for time off so soon."

"Late afternoon, I mean," Frank said. "I'm working, too. But I've rented a canoe for a week or so. It's moored on West Okoboji. How about going out for a short canoe ride after you close shop? We can be back at the lodge in time for dinner."

"All right," Ellen said. "But I don't know much about paddling a canoe."

"I know enough for both of us. I'll teach you."

Frank left his car in the parking lot at the lodge, and they strolled hand in hand to the front entrance. Pausing in the shadow of a fragrant honeysuckle vine, Frank kissed Ellen good night.

Once in her room Ellen moved about quietly as she prepared for bed. The rest of the lodge was dark and silent, and she didn't want to wake anyone whose room might be under hers. She tried to concentrate on the decision that faced her concerning her teaching job, but her thoughts kept returning to Frank — the touch of his hand, the protective feel of his arms, the warmth of his kiss. At last she turned out her bedside light and tried to sleep. She had not come here for a summer romance. She had tried to keep her mind on her private business and on helping Aunt Madeleine.

As Ellen lay awake she at first thought she was imagining things. Music at this hour of the night? Propping herself on one elbow, she listened. Music. There was no doubt about it. The sound was coming from somewhere near the lake. She got up and looked out the window. All was dark. Then she saw a flash of light. She might have imagined it, so quickly did it disappear. She strained her eyes, peering into the night, but all was dark.

Ellen's thoughts flew immediately to the newspaper article about the runaway girl. Was there a child down on that lakeshore tonight? She had to know. Slipping into her loafers, she pulled on jeans and a shirt and tiptoed to the steps.

Some of the stair treads creaked under her weight, but Ellen continued her descent. When she reached the parlor, she felt her way across the vast space to the rear door that opened onto the patio. Turning the key in the lock, Ellen opened the door and stepped into the night. Branches of the fallen oak blocked her way, and she stepped over and around them until she reached the steps leading to the lake.

The high retaining walls on either side of the steps shadowed her way, but Ellen followed the sound of the music, touching the retaining walls for support. When she reached the quay, she turned right. The music sounded louder now. Was someone trying to steal the rowboat? Or was someone trying to borrow it for a moonlight ride? The music was coming from under the willow branches.

A chill prickled Ellen's spine, and gooseflesh rose on her arms. She had been foolish to come here alone. Anyone could be hiding here in the dark. She thought of the boy she had seen hitchhiking as she and Frank drove to the Beachcomber. She was about to turn back to go to the lodge for help when a soft voice began singing along with the music. But what sort of voice was it? Male or female?

Ellen stiffened in anticipation when both the music and the voice suddenly ceased in the middle of a phrase. Instinctively she knew she had been seen. But by whom? It was too late to retreat now. Wtih a false show of bravery Ellen stepped forward and thrust the willow branches aside.

CHAPTER NINE

It took a moment for Ellen's eyes to adjust to the darkness under the willow branches; then she made out the form of the small girl hiding near the thick tree trunk.

"Lori? Lori Wilde?"

"How did you know my name?" The girl scrunched closer to the tree trunk, like a wild animal trying to avoid all contact with humans.

"I read it in the paper," Ellen said. "I guessed all along that you were hiding around here somewhere. You see, early yesterday morning I found your purple hair yarn upstairs in one of the unused bed-rooms."

"I suppose you're going to call the cops on me." Resignation and belligerence rasped in Lori's voice.

"Come out here where we can talk." Ellen lifted the willow branches higher. "I'm not in the habit of calling the cops on people, but there are some things we need to talk about. Come on out."

Lori crept from her hiding place and stood beside Ellen on the lakeshore with her feet widespread, her fists on her hips, and her chin jutted skyward. She was like a firecracker daring someone to light the fuse. Lori fitted her newspaper description; she still wore the cut-off jeans, the purple shirt, and the mismatched socks. Only a bare rubber band held her ponytail in place.

"Where have you been hiding?" Ellen asked, leading the way up the lodge steps to the first landing. Lori followed her until Ellen motioned her to sit down beside her on one of the cement benches. As she sat down Ellen smelled a spicy odor of cinnamon balls.

"Guess you know I've been hiding up on the third floor," Lori said. "Guess you know that from finding my hair yarn up there. Why are you bothering to ask me dumb questions?"

"But you weren't in the third-floor room the next time I went back to check — after I'd read the notice in the newspaper. Where were you then?"

Lori sighed. "There're a hundred empty rooms up there. That's why I picked this old place for my hideout. I used to hitchhike out here just to play before your aunt bought the place." Lori snorted. "It's not a whole lot different now than it was before she took over. Eight people in all those rooms! I knew I could get by with hiding out here."

"Hiding out must have been terribly boring," Ellen suggested. "And hot."

"Not really." Lori kicked at a pebble with her toe. "I only stayed inside during the daytime. And I slept then. At night I've been playing outdoors beside the lake." Lori's voice took on a faraway quality, almost as if she were talking to herself. "Nighttime is beautiful with the moon making everything look all shiny and new. Just like dumb grownups to spend the best time of day sleeping."

"What did you do at night?" Ellen asked.

"Sometimes I'd go rowing in the lodge boat, and sometimes I'd go fishing. Never caught anything, though. And sometimes I'd just sit and watch the water. Big Spirit never looks the same two seconds in a row. Did you know that?"

"Guess I'd never thought about it," Ellen said. "I'll notice after this. But what have you been living on? Eating, I mean? Are you hungry?"

"I'm hungry," Lori said. "Starving. You

got any food on you?"

Ellen stood. "No, but there's plenty of milk and sandwich makings in the lodge kitchen. Come on, you can talk to me while you eat."

"Nothing doing." Lori sat as if her hips had taken root to the concrete bench. "You're trying to trick me. You'll get me up there where people are, then you'll yell or something and that aunt of yours will call the cops. I can tell just by looking at her that she's the flighty type. Nervous as a hummingbird."

"Lori." Ellen waited until the child looked directly at her. "I'm not going to turn you in. That's a solemn promise. You can depend on it."

"Why?"

"A lot of reasons."

"Give me just one." Lori met Ellen's gaze, but she held her head tilted to one side as if she were half willing to listen.

"Once I was a runaway myself. I know how it is."

"You're a liar." Lori held her head so straight she could have balanced a book on it.

"I'm telling the truth," Ellen said. "But I was older than you when I ran away. I was fifteen. I guess it's easier to survive as a runaway when you're a little older. I took off from a foster home. But eventually I gave myself up."

"Why?"

Ellen squirmed and hesitated, planning her answer cautiously. Lori had a knack for directness that she herself often used. Such directness demanded an honest answer. "I gave myself up because I knew it was the smart thing to do. In time the authorities would have caught up with me, just as they'll catch up with you. But I had the satisfaction of knowing that I had done the right thing. I had made an important decision on my own."

"You're trying to talk me into something."

"Only if you're willing to be talked into it." Mentally Ellen cringed in guilt. If she was such a great decision maker, why hadn't she called the hospital board before this?

"Come on now, Lori. Let's go put something into your stomach. What have you been living on besides Josie's cherry pie?"

"How'd you know about that?" Lori held herself very still, and Ellen recognized the stillness as shock at having been discovered.

"Josie told me a pie had disappeared," Ellen said. "She didn't know who took it, though. She was blaming the wrong person. A runaway can drag a lot of innocent people into trouble. Come with me."

This time Lori stood and walked beside Ellen up the next flight of stairs. They entered the lodge noiselessly. Once in the kitchen Ellen got out an iron skillet and began scrambling some eggs.

"I like bacon, too," Lori said.

"Sorry. Not practical." Ellen grinned. "The smell. We'd have everyone waking up and running in here for a taste." Ellen poured Lori a glass of milk and made her some toast. Then she sat down at the table with her while she ate.

"Why did you run away from your foster home, Lori?" Ellen asked after Lori had had a chance to take a few bites of egg and toast. "Wasn't there anything about the Stone family that you liked?"

"A foster home is a whole lot like a jail," Lori said. "The cops might as well put bars across the windows and doors. Someone's watching you all the time. They pretend they aren't, but they are. In a foster home someone's thinking up chores for you to do all day long. And at every meal someone's watching to see how much you eat. I eat a lot. It surprises people. They don't like it."

"Was there nothing about the home that you liked?" Ellen repeated her question as she poured Lori a second glass of milk, then replaced the carton in the refrigerator. "Nothing at all that you liked?"

After a long time Lori answered. "There was an old lady lived there. She's really ancient — wrinkled like a prune. She's almost blind but not quite. She can see me, but she can't see to read or anything like that. She liked it when I'd read to her. The newspaper. Books. The Bible. She liked it a lot when I read to her from the Bible. And when I'd get tired of reading to her, she'd tell me legends."

"What sort of legends?" Ellen asked.

"Legends about the lakes," Lori said. "Neat legends about Indians and things. She was a nice old lady. I liked her. She wasn't like the rest of them. She didn't care how much I ate. She couldn't see to tell."

"I'll bet she misses you," Ellen said. "It's not too late to go back, you know."

Lori finished off the scrambled eggs and chewed on a toast crust. "Lady, I'm not going back. I can make it on my own. I don't need nobody else looking after me. Not for one minute do I need that. My mom and me, we're loners. We'll get by. As long as you don't sic the cops on me, I'll get by until —"

"Getting put in jail isn't my idea of a great life," Ellen said, hating to remind Lori of her mother, yet feeling the need to make a point.

"My mom was framed," Lori said. "Those dirty cops framed her all over the place. She told me she was innocent, and I believe her. My mom wouldn't lie to me."

"She was caught shoplifting," Ellen said. "According to the newspaper she had the merchandise in her possession outside the store. And she had no sales slip to prove that she'd paid for it."

"And you know what the merchandise was?" Lori demanded. "It was food. A loaf of hard-crust bread. A wedge of white cheese. Crackers. Mom has to steal because my chintzy dad doesn't send the support payments like he's supposed to. She had to do it. It's all my fault. She was stealing for me. She hates to see me hungry. I eat a lot."

"She could have tried getting a job," Ellen said.

"Mom did try." Lori's voice dropped to a hoarse whisper, and she looked at the floor. "But she never finished high school. Everyone says, 'Let's see your diploma,' and since she has no diploma to show, they say, 'Sorry, no job. Come back when you get your diploma.' But Mom's too old to get a diploma. That's for kids. She's almost thirty years old."

126

"Nobody's ever too old to go to school," Ellen said. "Never. Do you want anything else to eat?"

Lori shook her head. "No. I'm stuffed. My stomach feels good for a change."

"Why don't you spend tonight inside the lodge as my guest?" Ellen asked. "I'll find you a room with a bed in it. I'll find sheets —"

Lori shook her head. "I have a bed for the night. All I want is for nobody to turn me in to the cops the minute my back's turned."

"Where's your bed?" Ellen asked.

"Under the rowboat."

"So you're the one who flipped it over."

"Right. I saw that storm brewing after I left the lodge before sunrise this morning. But it was too late to come back inside. The cook was already here. And that guy who measures everything was already creeping around with his steel tape. So was the fellow with the clipboard who doesn't write very much on it. I knew it was going to rain, so I turned the boat over, and when the storm hit, I hid under it. I kept dry, too. Lots of excitement when the tree went down."

"Lots," Ellen agreed.

"When I heard the noise, I thought the cops had come for me and had fired off a gun. When I got up enough nerve, I peeked from under thc boat and saw the oak down. I breathed a lot easier then, I tell you."

"Please stay inside tonight," Ellen begged. "No one will have to know."

Lori shook her head and headed for the door. "And no use for you to call the cops. I'll have a new hiding place before they could ever get clear out here and scout around for me. I got lots of places lined up for emergency use. Lots."

Ellen followed Lori to the door. "You needn't worry. I gave you my promise. I'm not going to turn you in."

"Why?"

"I told you once. Because I know how it is to be a runaway."

"That's not good enough. Why else?"

"Because I think you're brave enough to turn yourself in when the time is right."

"You're nuts, lady."

"Won't you call me Ellen?"

"You're nuts, Ellen."

"Perhaps," Ellen admitted. "But I know you're brave. How many kids would even try to make it on their own if their mothers were in jail? I know you're brave, Lori, and I know you'll do the right thing. You think a lot of your mother, don't you?"

"You know I do."

"I also know that you won't want her to worry about you while she's locked up and can't do a thing to help you."

"Mom thinks I'm at the Stones', at the foster home."

"No, she doesn't," Ellen said. "Your mother will have read the newspapers by now. She may be in jail, but she'll have heard the radio newscasts. She's probably lying on her cot right this minute worrying about what's happened to you. She probably thinks thugs have kidnapped you. Mothers get strange ideas, you know. Or she may think you've been run over by a car."

Lori's scowl told Ellen that she was hitting home with her speculations. "But you go on and spend the night outdoors. It won't hurt your mother to worry a little as long as you're really safe."

"Maybe I should try to get in touch with her. Would they let me talk with her? Could anyone trace a telephone call?"

"I'll call for you if you want me to."

"Don't you dare, lady. You'll call the cops on me. I'll get in touch with Mom in my own way. And if you call the police, I'll run. I can run real, real fast. I'll swim clear across Big Spirit. They'll never catch me." Without waiting for more talk Lori took off at top speed and disappeared into the shadows by the lakeshore.

Slowly Ellen climbed the stairs to the second floor, letting the smooth banister guide her. Had she done the right thing? Why was it always so hard to know what was right! If she had turned Lori in, the child would only have run away again. And next time she might not run to such a safe spot as Scarlet Point.

If Ellen called the police to come get Lori, the child would be captured in defeat. How much better if she would turn herself in to the authorities as an act of personal bravery. Ellen knew she had planted the seed of an idea in Lori's mind. She would wait, give the seed time to sprout. In the meantime Lori was safe on the lodge grounds.

CHAPTER TEN

The next morning Ellen rose early and went for a walk along the shore. She tried to tell herself that she didn't expect to see Lori, but she did. When the child made no appearance, Ellen tried to tell herself that she had come here to be alone, to think.

In a way that was partly true. In only a few days she had to give her decision about Janey Van Allen to the hospital board, and she still didn't know what that decision was going to be. Maybe Frank was right. Maybe she should forget all about California. Maybe she should go to New York and start afresh. The hospital would go on without her, perhaps better without her than with her.

As she walked along, Ellen's thoughts turned to Frank and their evening together. She admired Frank. Clearly he was a man on his way up. He had his sights on far-distant goals, and if her guess was correct,

Frank would achieve them. New York. Frank would fit in there. Ellen had never been there, but from what she had heard and read she sensed that Frank would fit in.

Ellen tensed as she heard footsteps behind her. Lori? Suddenly Frank was walking beside her, matching his long stride to her shorter one.

"Out early," Frank commented. "Morning's a beautiful time of day in June."

"Frank! I was just thinking about you and about what a nice time I had last night." Ellen felt blood rush to her face. Frank would think her too eager. Why did she always blurt out her feelings!

"And I was thinking of you." Frank grinned down at her. "Must be ESP."

Ellen was pleased yet dismayed that Frank had joined her. She still rather hoped to see Lori Wilde somewhere in the vicinity of the willows or the quay. And she hoped that during the night Lori had changed her stubborn mind about hiding out from the authorities. But now that Frank had joined her the child would surely stay in hiding.

"You're shivering," Frank said. "Here, slip my sweater around your shoulders."

"I didn't realize it was so chilly out," Ellen said. "But I don't want you to be cold."

Frank draped his sweater around her

shoulders, and Ellen basked in its cashmere softness. Was Lori warm enough? Was she prepared for changes in the weather?

"The wind blowing out of the north and across the water can be brisk," Frank said. "But the sun'll soon warm things up. Since she has no air conditioning, your aunt is lucky that the temperature cools down at night."

"Frank, do you ever imagine what it would have been like to have lived here in a tent — or in a log cabin, as the early settlers did? Can you imagine a blizzard blowing across Big Spirit?"

"No," Frank replied. "I try not to let the past shackle my mind. I find it more to the point to try to imagine condominiums surrounding the lake. The right person could develop the real estate around Big Spirit and make a fortune."

"There's your chance," Ellen said. "Maybe Iowa could offer as many opportunities as New York."

"It's not for me," Frank said. "I told you. I'm on my way to the East Coast just as soon as I finish the work at Scarlet Point."

"Frank!" Ellen stopped and clutched at Frank's arm, pointing to the lodge. "Is that smoke pouring out the patio doorway?"

"It certainly looks like it." Frank grabbed

Ellen's hand, and they sprinted toward the lodge. Taking the steps two at a time, they raced across the patio. Frank jerked the door open. Aunt Madeleine and Mrs. Young came rushing across the parlor, coughing and fanning the air with folded newspapers. In the next second Judge Cloud burst through the doorway, wiping his eyes and wheezing

"It's the fireplace," Mr. Boast shouted to Frank as he followed the ladies and Judge Cloud outside. "She's smoking like a volcano, and the flue's blocked."

Gulping a deep breath, Frank ran across the parlor to the fireplace while Ellen helped the guests out onto the patio and settled them in lawn chairs. She loaned Frank's sweater to Miss Speer. "I'm sure everything will be all right in just a few minutes. The air is clear out here."

"The place is on fire," Miss Speer screeched. "All this excitement is not good for my high blood pressure."

"No, it isn't," Ellen said. "On fire, that is. It's just the fireplace. Something is wrong with the flue. We'll have it taken care of in a moment. Frank is seeing to it right now. He'll know what to do. Try to be calm."

"Take deep breaths," Mr. Boast advised.

"Oh, dear!" Aunt Madeleine exclaimed.

"Oh, dear me!"

In moments Frank appeared in the patio doorway. "Everything's all okay now, Mrs. Ferris. Someone just forgot to open the flue vent. It'll take a few minutes for the smoke to clear out, but there's no real damage done."

Aunt Madeleine broke into tears, hiding her face in her hands. Ellen ran to her side.

"What is it, Aunt Madeleine? What's the matter? Frank says everything is okay."

"This is all my fault." Aunt Madeleine choked on her sobs. "Everything I do is the wrong thing. I was only trying to make my guests comfortable. It was chilly this morning. You know it was. Down in the fifties. The parlor seemed cold and clammy, so I thought I'd start a fire in the fireplace. The logs were all laid." Aunt Madeleine dabbed at her nose with a lace handkerchief as mascara ran down her checks in black rivulets.

"Everything's going to be all right." Ellen patted her aunt on the arm. "Crying is not going to help. You're upsetting the guests."

"I didn't know I was supposed to open the flue," Aunt Madeleine wailed. "I don't even know where the flue vent is."

While Ellen was trying to calm her aunt, Josie appeared in the doorway. Her nose and cheeks were red, and her eyes were watering from the smoke. "How lucky that I've planned an early patio breakfast this morning, folks. If someone will pull the chairs up to the patio table and if someone else will round up some sweaters and jackets, I'll soon be ready to serve you."

"I'll take care of the chairs, Josie." Doug appeared behind Josie, and Ellen knew he had been helping her in the kitchen. What would Aunt Madeleine do without someone to bail her out of her troubles! At Ellen's suggestion her aunt hurried inside for sweaters.

Suddenly Ellen felt a tug on her sleeve. Turning, she faced Judge Cloud. He was choking and coughing. His chest was puffed up. His lips were blue. Ellen knew immediately that all the smoke had triggered an asthma attack.

"Come with me," Ellen ordered. She took the judge's arm and tried to lead him into the lodge.

"Not in there," Judge Cloud wheezed and pulled away from Ellen's grasp.

"But I have to get medication," Ellen said. "I can't help you out here."

"Medicine — in — my — room," Judge Cloud wheezed between coughs. "On — the — dresser."

"I'll get it for you," Doug said to Ellen. "Make him comfortable out here."

Ellen led Judge Cloud to a lounge chair away from the others and helped him ease himself into it and put his feet up. In moments Doug was back with the medicine and a glass of water.

Judge Cloud took one kind of medicine by mouth and inhaled another kind. Within five minutes his attack had subsided. But even after he could breathe freely again, Ellen insisted that he remain quiet and away from the others. She carried his breakfast to him on a tray, then joined him to eat while the other guests stayed around the patio table.

"I'm packing up and leaving this place just as soon as I eat," Judge Cloud said. "Madeleine Ferris is an idiot. This place isn't a vacation lodge, it's an . . . !" Judge Cloud spluttered, at a loss for words.

"Do try to be calm," Ellen said. "You don't want to bring on another asthma attack. Emotional turmoil can precipitate unfortunate events."

"So can smoke!" Judge Cloud tried to control himself. "But that woman!"

"Aunt Madeleine does the best she can, Judge Cloud. She's just inexperienced at managing a lodge. But isn't this breakfast wonderful? Aunt Madeleine was smart enough to hire the best cook in the area. Did you ever taste such delicious bran muffins? And try this fruit! Josie must be a favorite of all the green grocers. And I'm sure she makes the best coffee in Iowa."

Ellen's psychology worked. Judge Cloud was soon quietly enjoying the fresh fruit mixture Josie had blended, and within moments he asked for a second buttered muffin to go along with his second cup of coffee.

Ellen excused herself to go to the kitchen for more butter. "Josie!" she exclaimed. "You've saved Aunt Madeleine again. I'm glad there's at least one person around here who knows what she's doing. The guests have forgotten all about the smoke. They're absolutely raving over your breakfast."

"For some reason food always tastes better outside," Josie said modestly.

"You know that isn't the reason they're raving." Ellen laughed as she refilled the butter plate and indulged in half a muffin straight from the oven.

"The guests may be pleased at the moment," Josie said, "but they're going to go sour again when they come back inside. Most of the smoke has cleared, but the smell is still here. It'll take a while to get rid of that. Don't know what we're going to do with them for the morning. I've got sprays, air fresheners, but. . ."

Ellen had an idea. "Last night when I was out to dinner I saw an excursion boat on West Okoboji. Do you know anything about it? Does the captain require advance reservations?"

"The *Boji Queen?*" Josie shrugged. "I've seen the boat plenty of times. Never been on it, though."

"I wonder if it makes morning trips," Ellen said.

"Would guess that it does." Josie unplugged the coffee pot. "The money that's made here has to be made in a mighty short season. My guess is that the boat runs mornings. Why don't you call the captain and find out for sure?" Josie nodded toward the telephone, pulled out a directory, and handed it to Ellen.

Ellen turned to the yellow pages, running her finger down the list of names until she came to the *Boji Queen.* Dialing the number, she waited. For a moment she thought nobody was going to answer; then a voice shrilled across the wire. Ellen got the information she needed, smiled triumphantly at Josie, and hurried back to the patio.

"Aunt Madeleine and I have a surprise for you this morning," Ellen announced, smiling and winking at her aunt. "We're all going for a boat ride on West Okoboji. The *Boji Queen* will be waiting to take us aboard in just thirty minutes from now. There'll be music. There'll be dancing. There'll be a tour guide to point out special places of interest. Doug, if you can drive Aunt Madeleine's station wagon, we'll all go in the one car."

"Will do," Doug said. "I'll have it out front in five minutes."

"Everybody get ready," Ellen said. "Better take sweaters. You may need hats or scarves, too. But hurry. We don't want to be left behind."

As the guests went inside for a moment to prepare for their surprise boat ride, Aunt Madeleine approached Ellen. "You're a lifesaver, Ellen. I'll stay here. Maybe Josie and I can get the place aired out before you return."

"Why don't you come with us?" Ellen invited. "You need a little relaxation, too. I think Josie can take care of things here. We'll all eat lunch aboard the boat. She'll be spared that noon duty."

"No. I'll stay here this morning. Frank'll

be here, and sometimes he has questions about just what I want done. You and Doug go ahead with the guests. And, Ellen, I do appreciate what you're doing."

Ellen grinned. "First aid can sometimes be mental as well as physical. It's all in the line of duty."

Everyone laughed and joked on the short ride to the boat dock. Miss Speer had her binoculars slung around her neck, and Mr. Boast did deep-breathing exercises as they drove along. Mrs. Young complained that she would miss her favorite soap opera on TV, but she hushed when Miss Speer suggested that there might be a TV aboard the *Boji Queen.*

After Doug parked the car near the dock, he and Captain Carey of the *Boji Queen* helped the guests up the sloping gangplank. Ellen began to feel the excitement of the excursion. Or maybe she just felt the roll of the boat and the slap of the sharp morning breeze against her cheeks.

"This boat looks more like a floating birthday cake than anything else," Ellen said to Doug after they had the guests settled comfortably on the pink benches by the railing and on the shady side of the deck.

"The white paint and pink trim does give

141

a birthday-party effect." Doug laughed. "This was a great idea of yours. Hope everybody's happy."

"But everybody's not happy." Ellen sighed. "Here comes Miss Speer now."

"I want to go up on the top deck," Miss Speer said. "Can't bird-watch with this low roof blocking my view."

"Of course, Miss Speer," Doug said. "Come with me and I'll show you the way."

Ellen watched as Doug took Miss Speer's arm and helped her walk down the aisle between the observation benches, up the rather steep steps at the stern of the boat, and onto the top deck.

"Believe I'd like to go up there, too." Mr. Boast stood. "Maybe there's space enough to walk around, to get a little exercise."

Mr. Boast left, and Ellen sat quietly until Doug returned. "There's a jazz group playing on the lower deck, Ellen. Would you like to dance?"

"Do we dare?" Ellen asked. "It would be just my luck for someone to fall overboard while I wasn't watching."

"No way." Doug laughed as he took Ellen's hand and pulled her to her feet. "We left your aunt back at Scarlet Point, remember? She's the jinx in this outfit."

"Doug! That's unfair. Aunt Madeleine has

lots of good ideas. And she's trying to make all her guests comfortable and happy. She's just unsure of what she should do."

"That's an understatement if I ever heard one." Doug chuckled. "Come on, Ellen. Everyone's happy. Everyone's being entertained. Judge Cloud is busy talking to Mrs. Young. She may decide that real people are more interesting than soap operas before the ride's over."

Ellen went with Doug down narrow steps. Glass windows enclosed the lower deck with its snack booths and dance floor. The smell of cigarette smoke and diesel exhaust hung all around them, and Ellen felt the warm, stale air against her cheeks. A few other couples sat at the booths that surrounded the dance area, but Doug led Ellen to the middle of the floor, where they waited for the music to begin.

Three musicians dressed in pink coats, pink shirts, and white slacks took their places on a small bandstand.

"Piano, bass, and drums," Doug said. "My favorite combination of instruments." He took Ellen in his arms as the music began, and they danced, oblivious to the gentle rocking of the boat. Doug was a good dancer. When the set ended, the observers applauded. Ellen felt her face flush, and she reached up to smooth her hair into place.

"Didn't know we were the floor show," Ellen said, grinning up at Doug. "Guess I was lost in the music."

"Let's sit the next set out and give some other couples a chance at the dance floor." Doug led Ellen to a booth and ordered lemonades. After they had quenched their thirst, Ellen began to squirm and glance at her watch.

"I'd better go check on our guests, Doug. I wouldn't want anything else to happen to them this morning. Seems strange that not one of them has ventured down here."

Doug nodded and they climbed the narrow steps to the first deck. Gratefully Ellen inhaled the fresh air. Judge Cloud and Mrs. Young were still visiting.

"Let's go on up to the top deck," Doug said. "We'd better see how the other two are doing."

On the open top deck the wind freshened. Ellen felt it paste her dress to her body and blow her hair into a tangle. Mr. Boast had relaxed in a deck chair with his back to the breeze, and Miss Speer stood beside him, scanning the horizon with her binoculars.

For a while Ellen watched the passing scene without speaking while she listened to the wind rush past her ears. Oaks and willows shaded the shoreline, almost blocking the view of the elegant homes that surrounded the lake. Children played tag in the shallows. Couples sunbathed on narrow wooden docks. And here and there speedboats towed water-skiers.

"What do you want from life, Ellen?" Doug asked suddenly. "What big thing do you really want?"

Ellen thought for a moment and wished she could avoid answering. "I've never considered it seriously, Doug. At least not out loud. I just want to do my very best for my nursing school and for the hospital where I work." She paused for a moment. "That doesn't sound like much, does it? Guess I'm a low-key sort of person when it comes to goals and ambitions."

Doug grinned at her. "It sounds like quite a bit to me. In a broad sense you might say you're devoting your life to protecting the dignity of man. What could be more important than that?"

Ellen laughed. "Better be careful or you'll give me delusions of grandeur. What's your big thing? Turnabout is only fair. What do you want from life?"

Ellen saw Doug's face flush as he replied, "Don't laugh."

"I won't laugh."

"Okay. I want to make some ordinary place special by writing about it. You know — some of the great writers have done it. Of course, the place would really be special. I would just sort of point it out to folks in a meaningful way."

"That's a big order," Ellen said.

"It's a goal that could be accomplished through art. Every place in the world is special, but life moves so fast that it takes a magician, or an artist, to make people stop and notice the uniqueness right at their doorstep."

Ellen looked at Doug with fresh understanding. In a few words he had explained the unrest that she felt within him, for surely such a goal would make a person restless. In a few moments Doug had drawn her to him, made her see a new facet of his personality. Suddenly she had a desire to tell Doug about Lori Wilde. But in the next moment she squelched the desire. Lori was her problem, not Doug's.

CHAPTER ELEVEN

It was midafternoon when the excursion-boat party returned to Scarlet Point. Aunt Madeleine and Josie had aired out the lodge, and it smelled sweet and fresh. The guests seemed contented to go to their rooms for a rest, and Ellen was ready to take a breather, too.

Stretched across her bed with her shoes off and two pillows under her head, Ellen thought about Frank and Doug. How different they were! One moment she was deeply attracted to Frank and all his suave smoothness. And the next moment she felt drawn to Doug and his restless probing to the heart of things. All at once she remembered the late-afternoon date with Frank. She had almost forgotten. This was the day she had promised to go canoeing with him.

Jumping up from her bed, Ellen hurried downstairs to the kitchen, hoping she would have it to herself. But no. Josie was defrosting the refrigerator.

"Josie, would you mind if I made a sandwich?"

"Help yourself, Miss Ellen. Or I'll do it for you if you'll let me." Josie carried a pan of ice across the room and dumped it into the sink.

"No, no, you're too busy. I'll do it." Ellen got out the bread and butter.

"They didn't feed you well on the *Boji Queen?*"

"Oh, the lunch was good. Excellent. I guess being out on the water just gave me an extra big appetite."

Ellen's earlobes always turned red when she lied, and she felt them burning right then. But it was just a tiny white lie. She did have a big appetite; that much was true. When she finished making the sandwich, she tucked it into a plastic bag and filled a tumbler with milk.

"Thanks loads, Josie." Ellen smiled at the cook, then headed back upstairs.

Leaving the snack in her room, Ellen climbed to the third floor and began searching for Lori. Now that the child knew Ellen hadn't turned her in, surely she wouldn't have hidden herself so carefully. Ellen opened fifteen doors before she found Lori asleep on a bare mattress in a tiny room hardly larger than a walk-in closet. The window was closed; the room was hot. Lori's hair was damp with perspiration.

Ellen closed the door carefully and hurried back to her own room for the sandwich and milk. When she returned to Lori, the child was still sleeping. She needs the rest, Ellen thought. I'll leave the snack here where she'll find it when she wakes up.

Setting the sandwich and milk on a chair near the bed, Ellen opened the window a crack before she tiptoed from the room and hurried back downstairs.

"Ellen!" Aunt Madeleine met Ellen on the second-floor landing. "Whatever were you doing poking around on the third floor? It's like an oven up there. There's nothing wrong, is there?"

"Nothing at all, Aunt Madeleine. I just went up to see if all the smoke had cleared out or if we needed to open some windows." Ellen felt her earlobes burning again. "But everything smells fresh and clean. You and Josie did a good job of airing out."

"Ellen! Guess what! We have a new guest!" Aunt Madeleine's eyes sparkled as she imparted the news.

Ellen relaxed as her aunt changed the subject. "Come on into my room and tell me about her," Ellen invited. "Or is the new one a he?"

"Have you time to listen?" Aunt Madeleine swooped into Ellen's room without waiting for a reply.

Ellen glanced at her watch. "Plenty of time. I'm going canoeing with Frank in a few minutes, but do sit down and talk to me while I change into my swimsuit and a cover-up. Who is the new one? Does he or she have any special health problems?"

Ellen went to the closet to select her outfit, and Aunt Madeleine moved to the dressing table and idly began repairing her makeup while Ellen changed clothes. Aunt Madeleine seemed to lose interest in the new guest as she focused her attention on her niece.

"I'm glad you're going out with Frank, Ellen. It's time you began thinking of marriage. Frank is a thoroughly nice person, and he's a hard worker. He's given this job at Scarlet Point his full attention, and I really appreciate that. You could do a lot worse than Frank Welborn, Ellen."

"Aunt Madeleine! Didn't you promise no matchmaking? Besides, I'm sure Frank has lots of girl friends. We're just going canoeing. It's no big deal."

"What makes you say that about the girl friends?"

"Because he knows his way around so well. Head waiters know his favorite wine vintage. Waitresses smile and call him by name. The bandleader at the Beachcomber even knew his favorite tunes. You can't tell me he goes to the Beachcomber alone."

"Frank is an attractive man. No doubt he does have other girl friends, but . . ." Aunt Madeleine held out her right hand and examined her nails.

"No *buts,*" Ellen said. "Frank and I are just casual friends. You were going to tell me about your new guest, remember? Give."

Aunt Madeleine turned to face Ellen. "She's young. Really young. Younger than you, I'd guess. And she's alone. I'm really sort of worried about her. I don't think she's going to find compatible friends here at Scarlet Point. The age gap, you know."

"Where's she from? What's her name?" Ellen ran a comb through her straight hair, only half hearing her aunt's words.

Aunt Madeleine looked puzzled. "Would you believe that I don't know her name? I just saw her from a distance. Josie checked her in and showed her to a room. Lucky we had one made up and ready."

"Aunt Madeleine!" Ellen turned and gave her aunt her full attention. "You mean to tell me there's a new guest here and you don't know who she is or where she's from?"

Aunt Madeleine shrugged. "I can find out easily enough. She registered at the desk when she checked in. Want me to run downstairs and see?"

"Don't make a special trip," Ellen said. "We can check the register when I go down to meet Frank. But you did see her, didn't you? What does she look like? I think it's strange that a young girl would come here all alone unless she's in trouble of some sort." Another runaway? Ellen didn't suggest that to her aunt. No use looking for trouble.

"The girl looked tired," Aunt Madeleine said. "She has blonde hair and a good figure. She's about medium height, and she drives a pink convertible. Prettiest car I've ever seen. Makes me think she must be someone real special."

Ellen dropped her lipstick and scrambled after it. A pink convertible! It couldn't be. She tried to keep calm. "Cars don't make people special, Aunt Madeleine. Where's the girl now?"

"As I said, she's in her room. Sleeping, probably. She seemed terribly tired. Josie offered her a late lunch, but she refused. She asked not to be disturbed before dinner. That's why I haven't met her."

Ellen shoved a comb and lipstick into her shoulder purse, grabbed some suntan lotion and a kerchief for her hair, then paused by the door. "Ready, Aunt Madeleine? I don't want to keep Frank waiting."

"Nor do I want you to." Aunt Madeleine winked at Ellen, then peered into the mirror and tucked one curl in place before she followed Ellen from the room.

When they reached the first floor, Josie called Aunt Madeleine to the kitchen, but Ellen hurried to the reception desk, opened the drawer, and pulled out the register book. Turning through the pages, she stopped at the fresh entry scrawled across two lines in a bold script.

"Janey Van Allen," Ellen whispered to herself. "Why has she come here?"

"Talking to yourself?" Frank strode into the parlor and stepped to the desk. Peering over Ellen's shoulder, he gazed at the register book.

"This is enough to make anyone talk to herself." Ellen pointed to the name, which seemed to grow larger every time she looked at it.

"Janey Van Allen? Who's she?"

"Oh, Frank! Don't you remember? She's one of my nursing students from California. The one I caught cheating on the exam.

153

Why has she come here? I have nothing more to say to her. I don't want to see her."

"No doubt Janey wants to plead her cause one more time," Frank said. "She really must be serious about the nurse's training if she's driven all the way from the West Coast just to talk with you."

"If she was serious about becoming a nurse, she wouldn't have cheated on the exam, would she? She knew the consequences. She chose —"

"Maybe there were extenuating circumstances."

"Cheating is cheating." Ellen felt like stamping her foot to punctuate her remark, but she refrained. "If you're ready, let's go before Janey shows up and spoils our plans."

"Fine with me. Let's be off."

They started out the door; then Ellen turned. "Wait just a minute, Frank. I haven't had the first-aid center open all day. I should leave the key with Josie just in case someone needs something while we're gone. Aunt Madeleine might not be able to find her key in an emergency."

Ellen returned to her room, got the key, and gave it to the cook. Then they were off. For the first time Ellen really noticed Frank. His white swim trunks and terry robe were a perfect foil for his bronze suntan. Ellen knew she was thinking in cliches, but Frank did look like a Greek god — or maybe a quarterback for the Packers.

Frank drove to West Okoboji and parked near the boat dock. He took two canoe paddles and two flotation cushions from the car trunk, and as they walked out onto the wooden dock Ellen smiled up at him. She didn't intend to let Janey Van Allen spoil this outing.

"It's the blue canoe, isn't it?" Ellen asked.

"How'd you know?"

"It suits you. Matches your eyes and all that. Blue really is your color."

"That why you wore a blue suit and beach robe?" Frank teased.

Ellen grinned.

Frank tossed the cushions onto the canoe seats before he helped Ellen into the canoe and handed her a paddle. "You get the front seat and the short paddle. I'll sit in back and guide us. Okay?"

"Okay with me, but you'll have to tell me what to do."

Frank eased himself into the canoe, and though it wobbled, it didn't tip. He shoved them away from the dock with the tip of his paddle.

"Just keep paddling on the right side of the canoe," Frank said. "Keep your left hand high on the paddle and your right hand down fairly low. I'll head us toward a special cove I know about."

Ellen relaxed, feeling sure that Frank knew how to manage the canoe safely. She watched minnows darting about in the clear water, and she listened to the splash of gentle waves against the sides of the aluminum boat. Sometimes she pulled up strings of green moss on the end of her paddle, but when they got into deeper water, these disappeared.

"Now paddle on the other side," Frank instructed. "We need to make a turn."

Ellen changed sides with the paddle, dripping the cool water on her feet as she did so. They soon reached the cove Frank had mentioned.

"A sand beach, Frank. How nice!" Ellen waited until Frank eased the canoe onto the sand; then she stepped out, carrying the paddle with her. Frank tugged the canoe farther up onto the beach.

"Like to swim?" he asked.

"Love to. I've been around the water all day long; it's high time I got into it."

Frank waded into the water first and Ellen followed, feeling the satin coolness of the waves as they splashed against her skin. They swam. They floated. They back paddled.

"Race you to that raft." Frank nodded to a red and white platform mounted on oil drums that floated several hundred feet to their left.

"Lead the way." Ellen started off doing a strong crawl, but she soon changed to a sidestroke. Frank beat her easily, but she didn't care. How good it was to swim again! She suddenly realized how much she missed California and its sea-swept beaches.

They lay sunning themselves on the raft for a long time before Frank spoke.

"Ellen?"

"What?"

"Why don't you come with me to New York?"

"And do what?"

"And pursue your career there in the city. New York has super hospitals. It has good nursing schools. I can tell that this Van Allen girl is worrying you. Don't let her do it. Take off. It's easy once you make up your mind to do it."

"You make it sound so simple."

"It is simple. All you have to do is make the decision to leave California, to take charge of your own life. New York is big. You can be big with it. New York will make you whatever you want to be if you'll just give it half a chance. Think about it and let me know, Ellen."

Frank leaned over and kissed Ellen, and for a dazzling moment his plan seemed to make sense. She could be persuaded to leave California. The world wouldn't come to an end if one nursing instructor changed jobs. And Frank would help her. He knew his way around. Big cities and lots of people would never frighten Frank.

"Race you back," Frank said, breaking into Ellen's serious thoughts.

Suddenly Ellen had grave misgivings. What would she do in New York City if she couldn't find a teaching job? Where would she go?

"What's the matter, Ellen? You can make it back to the beach, can't you? If you're too tired, I'll swim back and pick you up in the canoe."

Ellen forced a smile. "I can swim back." How could Frank have his mind on asking her to go to New York with him and at the same time be thinking about swimming? Had she dreamed she heard that invitation? Or maybe Frank was already sorry he had spoken out. They hardly knew each other.

Ellen plunged into the water, and its coolness calmed her. Of course she wouldn't go to New York. It was an outlandish idea. It was the same thing as running away. She had been thinking off the top of her head to even consider such a plan. She wouldn't mention it again unless Frank did. Or should she? He had asked her to let him know.

They reached the sand beach puffing and dripping. Ellen splashed from the water and dropped down on a log to rest. Frank peered at his watch.

"Hey, would you believe it's almost dinner time? Of course, we could eat out."

"In swimsuits?" Ellen asked. "No. We should go back to the lodge. Josie is expecting us. We can't leave her holding a meal. It wouldn't be fair."

"You're right." Frank smiled. "You're always looking out for the other fellow, Ellen. It's an admirable trait. I like it. I just thought you might want to delay facing Janey Van Allen."

Frank eased the canoe parallel to the shore and waited for Ellen to climb in. When she was settled, he pushed them out to deeper water, then climbed onto the back seat. They began to paddle back toward the dock, taking their time, enjoying the scenery. Ellen heard the speedboat first and peered over her shoulder.

"Someone's coming up fast, Frank."

Frank shrugged. "We're to the right; we're out of the way. Anyway, whoever it is can surely see us. That's one reason why I rented a bright-blue boat. Safety factor."

Ellen went on paddling, but she felt more and more uneasy as the speedboat moved closer. "I don't like the way that guy's handling his boat," she shouted to Frank.

"Don't worry," Frank yelled above the roar of the speedboat's motor. "We have the right-of-way."

Ellen looked over her shoulder once more. "Frank! That guy doesn't see us. He's going to hit us."

"You're right," Frank yelled. "Jump. Swim away from the canoe toward the shore. Jump!"

Ellen jumped at the same time Frank did, swimming with powerful strokes to try to pull clear of the canoe. In seconds she heard the speedboat ram the canoe. Surfacing a few feet away, Ellen shook the water from her eyes in time to see the canoe fly through the air and the speedboat go on without stopping.

Ellen gasped all the air she could and did a dead man's float until the wake from the speedboat subsided. When she opened her eyes again, she saw Frank a few feet away.

"Are you okay?" Frank called.

She nodded. "Are you?"

"I'm fine." Frank scowled. "That guy must be drunk. I'm going to report him. Are you sure you're okay?"

"Okay, but badly shaken," Ellen called, swimming closer to Frank. "I think your canoe is ruined."

"You swim on to shore if you're sure you can make it," Frank said. "I'll tow what's left of the canoe in. It won't sink."

"I'll help you," Ellen said. "If we get tired, we can hang on to the canoe."

Together they managed to get the canoe back to the shore. Frank paced around it, examining it from all angles. Flopping down on the sand, Ellen thought she had never been so tired in all her life. She didn't have the strength to go back to Scarlet Point and face Janey Van Allen. She didn't want to do anything but rest for a long, long time. She lay back in the sand and closed her eyes until she heard feet pounding toward them.

"Are you two all right?" Doug called. "I saw what happened as I was driving along in my car. You had the right-of-way. I got that guy's registration number."

"Doug!" Ellen exclaimed. "What are you doing here?"

"I was just passing by on my way back to the lodge. I thought I recognized you two. I was going to honk and wave when that maniac started heading toward you. Can I be of any help?"

Frank shook his head. "There's no hope for the canoe. It's a mess. And I've got my car right over there." Frank pointed to the parking lot. "Nothing wrong with it."

"We may be here for a while," Ellen said. "You might tell Josie we'll be a little late — to go ahead and start dinner without us."

"Okay," Doug said. "Will do."

Doug gave them a farewell wave, and although Ellen turned to face Frank and the wrecked canoe, her mind was on Doug. Had he been following them, watching them? It seemed almost too much of a coincidence to have him passing by just at the moment they had been wrecked. Ellen supposed she should feel irritated at being spied upon, but she didn't. She found it rather flattering to know that Doug was interested in her.

CHAPTER TWELVE

Although it was well past eating time when Frank and Ellen got back to the lodge, they found that Josie had insisted on waiting dinner until they arrived. The guests crowded around them at the front doorway, eager to hear their version of the tale they had already heard from Doug.

"The canoe is ruined," Frank said, "but we weren't hurt. That's the important thing. Ellen is a strong swimmer, and neither of us was hurt. We were very lucky."

"You always were a good swimmer, Ellen," Aunt Madeleine said. "Those good summer camps I sent you to paid off in full measure, as I knew they would. Why, in a way I'm responsible for saving your life."

Ellen didn't feel like talking, but she managed to smile at her aunt's logic as she dragged herself upstairs to change into fresh clothes. How she wished she could skip dinner entirely and go straight to bed. She was bone tired. And she hated the thought of facing Janey Van Allen. But no. She must appear at the dinner table out of respect for Josie if for no other reason. If they lost Josie's help, Scarlet Point Lodge would fold around their ears.

Easing through the crowd once again, Ellen returned to the reception desk to see if she had any mail. The mailman arrived late in the afternoon, and she knew she had been out with Frank when he had made today's delivery. She felt guilty about taking the time when dinner was waiting, but she thought she might have a letter from the hospital board — a reprieve of some sort. And if she did, she wanted to read it before she faced Janey Van Allen.

There were three letters in the mail basket. Ellen couldn't help noticing that one of them was for Doug and that it was from a woman — a Julie Jackson. But Doug's correspondence was none of her business. Her shoulders slumped as she saw there was no letter for her.

Ellen managed to appear for dinner, managed to eat, and managed to visit casually with the guests for a few moments afterward. To her relief Janey Van Allen had not yet made an appearance. But just as Ellen thought she was going to be able to escape to the solitude of her room, Janey appeared in the doorway of the dining room. Aunt Madeleine rose to greet her, but instead of introducing her to everyone at the dinner table she motioned to Ellen to join them in an alcove off the parlor.

Ellen took her time excusing herself and leaving the dining room. All the while she studied Janey from the corner of her eye. Janey hadn't changed. But why should she have changed? It was less than a week ago that Ellen had seen her in the classroom. This evening her heart-shaped face looked tired and drawn, and her wheat-colored hair seemed less silky than usual. But the petal-colored shift she wore still gave her the pampered-in-pink look that was her trade-mark. If Janey wore perfume, Ellen felt sure it must smell like new dollar bills.

"I'm terribly sorry to barge in on you like this, Miss Ferris," Janey said as Ellen joined her in the alcove. "But I simply have to talk to you one more time before . . . You haven't called the hospital board yet, have you?"

Ellen shook her head. "No. I've reached no decision on the matter yet."

"Why don't you two talk in the first-aid rooms?" Aunt Madeleine suggested. "You can close the door and visit in private for as long as you need to."

Ellen smiled her thanks to her aunt. In practical matters Aunt Madeleine didn't quite make it, but socially she was definitely on top of every situation. Ellen hadn't wanted to invite Janey to her room; nor had she wanted to have this talk in Janey's quarters. The first-aid center was the ideal place — impersonal and cool.

"Did you have a good trip?" Ellen asked when she was seated behind her desk and Janey was perched on a chair in front of it.

"A tiring trip," Janey said. "The road is always long when one has a heavy burden."

Oh, can the dramatics! Ellen cleared her throat and waited for Janey to continue. This meeting was Janey's idea, and Ellen intended to let Janey manage it.

"I came here to ask you to let me continue my nurse's training," Janey said. "It's as simple as that. I'm begging."

"You know the rules," Ellen said. "We've been all over this before."

"Cheating is punishable by expulsion," Janey said, "but at the request of the teacher. I'm asking you to be lenient in my case. I'm asking that you petition the board on my behalf — ask them to let me continue."

"For what reason?" Ellen asked. "Why do you feel you should receive special favors?"

166

"I've admitted to the cheating," Janey said. "But I didn't tell you my reasons for cheating. I thought knowing the why of my action might make a difference in your decision. Will you listen?"

Knowing the why. Always more important than knowing the how. "I am listening."

"Three days before that final exam my younger sister became ill," Janey said. "She had a severe case of tonsillitis. Raging fever, sore throat, earache. My mother was out of town caring for my grandmother, who just recently had a stroke. I stayed home from classes to care for my sister. She's only seven years old."

"Why wasn't your sister in the hospital?" Ellen asked. "If she was that sick . . ."

"You should know the answer to that one." Janey eased back in her chair. "No beds available. I saw no point in insisting that she be allowed a bed out in the halls somewhere when I could care for her adequately at home. I'd had enough nurse's training to follow the doctor's orders. Anyway, there was little time for studying during those three days when Susie was so sick. And when there was time, I was so tired I would fall asleep over my books."

"I can understand that," Ellen said.

"Then maybe you can understand the

parental pressure I'm under. I hope so. I've always made good grades. With study I could have passed that exam with an easy A. Both my parents expect me to make top grades. Only top grades are in keeping with the family name, to hear them tell it. But I'll not blame anyone but myself. I knew better, yet I cheated. But I want you to know that if you give me another chance, it won't happen again. I promise you that."

"Somehow I believe you, Janey," Ellen said. "But that doesn't change things very much, does it?"

"I suppose not." Janey stood and paced the small room. "I'm concerned for that hospital, Miss Ferris. If I'm expelled, my father'll withhold his annual donation. The hospital and innocent patients will suffer, and all because of me."

"I'm afraid that's true," Ellen said. "Every effect has it's cause."

"Then you won't be persuaded in my favor?" Janey's eyelids drooped, and she looked very tired.

"I didn't say that. I haven't made my decision yet. You'll be the first to know when I do." Ellen stood to bring the interview to an end. There was no point in talking any longer. Nothing more remained to be said.

"I'm staying here at Scarlet Point until I

know what your decision is," Janey said. "Your aunt, Mrs. Ferris, says I may stay as long as I care to. She seems to have plenty of accommodations and no waiting list."

"Yes. I'm sure there'll be plenty of room for you for as long as you want to stay. And I do appreciate your coming to talk with me, Janey. Thank you."

"Being a nurse means a lot to me, Miss Ferris. My father is wealthy. You know that. But the right to serve people as a registered nurse is one thing Dad can't buy for me. My nurse's diploma is the one thing I'll have to earn for myself. And I want to earn it."

Ellen felt near collapse before Janey finally left her alone. The previous pressure she had felt concerning the hospital situation was minor compared to what she felt now. But in spite of herself she was impressed with Janey Van Allen, more impressed than she had been with her all year long in the classroom.

Janey had taken precious vacation time to drive halfway across a continent to plead her case. She had expressed genuine concern for the hospital, and her inborn instinct for nursing had led her to care for her sister in a time of emergency rather than turning her over to a crowded hospital. All those things would have to be taken into consideration. But Ellen could think no more about it tonight. Maybe tomorrow morning when her mind was fresh she could face the problem again. Tomorrow was her day off. Maybe she could think all day long.

It was dark and the moon was just rising when Ellen left the first-aid room. She slipped out the patio door and hurried down the steps toward the lake. On a hunch she headed toward the overturned rowboat. If Lori was willing to talk to her, surely she would make herself available now that it was dark and there was nobody else around.

"Lori," Ellen called softly. "Lori, it's me. Ellen. Are you here?"

For a moment she heard only crickets and frogs. Then a rustling in the leaves caught her attention, and Lori's head appeared in an opening of willow branches near the spot where the rowboat was hidden.

"Thanks for not turning me in, lady," Lori said. "Thanks a lot. I like people I can trust. And thanks for the food. I found it when I woke up, and I ate it."

"Please call me Ellen."

"Okay, Ellen. Thanks a lot."

"I really hated living off the land," Lori said. "Know what I've been eating?"

"What?"

"Wild asparagus. Raw. Have you ever eaten wild asparagus raw?"

"No," Ellen admitted. "But I suppose it's good for you."

"Yuck! It tastes terrible. I don't even like asparagus when it's cooked. Slimy."

"Lori, tomorrow's my day off, and in the morning I'll take you back to the Stones' house if you want to go. Just for a visit, of course."

"Will they lock me up?"

"I don't think so. They'll just be glad you came back willingly. How about it? I'll bet old Mrs. Stone misses your reading to her."

Lori thought for a minute. "If I went back, Mom would know about it, wouldn't she?"

"I'm sure she would. It would be on the radio and in the newspaper."

"Okay. I'll go. But just for the day. If they try to lock me up, I'll escape. I'll run away again."

Ellen thought fast, not knowing how all this was going to work out. She chose her words carefully. She didn't want to promise things she couldn't deliver, but neither did she want to scare Lori off.

"All right, Lori. I'll invite you back here as my guest for the evening tomorrow night. How's that?"

"That's a deal." Lori stood up to shake

hands. "Do you think they'll let me talk with my mother?"

"I can't promise you that," Ellen said. "But you can always ask. At least someone will get word to your mother that you're okay. That's what you really want, isn't is?"

Lori nodded.

"How about sleeping inside tonight?" Ellen invited. "I can sneak you upstairs and nobody will know."

Lori shook her head. "No thanks, lady. I slept all day. I can make it out here on my own. If you try to take me inside, I'll run. I'll see you in the morning."

Silently and quickly Lori disappeared into the undergrowth near the willows, leaving Ellen alone. She walked along the quay for several minutes, trying to reach a decision about Janey Van Allen, but the correct answer to the situation still eluded her. Somehow to say "Okay, Janey, all is forgiven" seemed too pat. Surely she could do better than that. But not tonight. She needed rest and sleep.

"Ellen?" Doug called. "Is that you? I've been looking all over for you."

"I've been out walking," Ellen said.

"Are you sure you're okay — after this afternoon, I mean? You had a narrow escape."

In the moonlight Ellen saw Doug's eyes glow, and she sensed an inner excitement driving him.

"But a narrow escape is just as effective as a wide escape." Ellen grinned. "I'm fine. I just feel sorry about the canoe. It was so pretty, and Frank thought a lot of it. I suppose the rental agency had it insured, though."

"No doubt it was the largest canoe on the lake," Doug said, sarcasm creeping into his voice.

Ellen chuckled. "Perhaps."

"Enough about Frank. I want to know if you'll spend tomorrow with me. I heard your aunt say it's your day off. Maybe you haven't had time to realize that yet."

Ellen stepped closer to Doug as he linked his arm through hers and walked on down the quay. "As a matter of fact I had realized it. It is my day off. Aunt Madeleine promised." Ellen smiled to herself. How could she say, "But I can't go out with you, Doug, because tomorrow's my day for thinking about Janey Van Allen"?

"You need a day off," Doug said. "We can visit that museum I was telling you about. And Josie promised me she'd make us a picnic lunch if I could talk you into going with me. Also, going out with me will get you away from Janey Van Allen, in case that would please you."

"I'd like to go with you, but there's just one thing."

"Don't tell me Frank has booked you up again!"

"No. Nothing like that." Ellen paused, then blurted out her story about Lori Wilde.

"You mean you've been hiding that kid from the authorities?" Doug asked. "Don't you know you can get into big trouble?"

"I didn't hide her," Ellen insisted. "She hid herself. I just didn't turn her in. I wanted her to give herself up, to do the brave thing, so she could like herself afterward. Can you understand that?"

Doug started up the steps leading back to the lodge. "Okay. I'll buy that. And I'll take you and Lori to the Stone home first thing tomorrow. Right after breakfast. Then we'll be on our way. Okay?"

"It's a deal," Ellen agreed.

Doug kissed Ellen good night at the patio door, and as Ellen walked up the curving staircase to her room she wondered about him. He had seemed to glow with an inner excitement tonight. At first she thought she might have inspired the glow, but then she remembered the letter Doug had received. Maybe Julie Jackson was the girl who turned

Doug on. But at least Ellen was looking forward to their day together tomorrow.

CHAPTER THIRTEEN

Although Ellen took a sunrise walk along the lakeshore the next morning, she saw nothing of Lori. Had the child changed her mind about returning to her foster home? Ellen hoped not. It was early. Lori had observed the lodge schedule carefully enough to know that Ellen wouldn't be leaving until after breakfast.

Returning to her room, Ellen packed her swimsuit and a towel in her beach bag and dressed in casual clothes. Then she undressed and slipped the swimsuit on and put the clothes on over it. There might be no handy place to change at the lake. Gathering suntan lotion, comb, and insect repellent, she tried to occupy her mind with small things in order to free it from the larger things like Lori Wilde and Janey Van Allen.

Everyone was present at the breakfast table, and Ellen noticed that Frank made it a point to sit by Janey, who looked refreshed after a night's sleep. Doug sat across from Ellen and took his gaze from her only in order to eat.

Aunt Madeleine cleared her throat. "I want everyone to know that today is Ellen's day off. If you have first-aid needs, please see me and I'll do what I can for you. The first-aid center will be locked, but I have a key. Don't hesitate to call on me."

"What are you going to do with your day off?" Mr. Boast asked.

"I thought I'd see some of the local sights," Ellen answered evasively.

"I know where there's a gymnasium if you want to get a good workout," Mr. Boast said.

"Maybe she'd prefer a quiet day of TV." Mrs. Young scowled at Mr. Boast. "Everyone doesn't have to be on the go every minute, you know."

Ellen was glad when breakfast ended and she could escape from the curious eyes and the well-meaning suggestions. When she and Doug stepped out the front door of the lodge, Lori was waiting behind a spruce tree. When she saw Doug, she ducked behind sheltering branches.

"He's okay, Lori," Ellen said. "Come on out. He's a friend of mine, Doug Cooper. He's going to drive you to the Stone home, and then we're going to visit a museum."

Reluctantly Lori joined them on the short walk to Doug's car. She frowned. "I want you to let me out about a block from the house. Okay?"

"Don't you want me to go with you to face Mrs. Stone?" Ellen asked when they were under way. "There's going to be some explaining to do."

"I can speak for myself," Lori said. "No use getting you involved in this. Mrs. Stone will just call the social worker, and she'll come talk to me and say, 'Naughty, naughty girl.' I've been all through this before. I can take care of myself."

Doug turned the car onto the highway, and Ellen waited a few moments before she spoke again. "What about tonight, Lori?"

"You promised you'd come get me."

"I promised I'd invite you to spend the night at Scarlet Point," Ellen reminded. "And I will. But what if Mrs. Stone doesn't want you to leave? That's a strong possibility. I can't take you without her consent."

Lori squirmed on the car seat between them. "I think Mrs. Stone'll let me go. I'll tell the social worker you're my good friend and that you're going to invite me. Is that okay?"

"Of course I'm your good friend," Ellen

said. "That would be the truth. And I have invited you. But what if they say you can't visit? You know, your record's not so good, not since you ran away, not since you've worried everyone so."

"I won't stay there overnight," Lori said. "I won't. And that's final. If they won't let me visit you, I'll run away again. But you'll come for me, won't you? They won't believe I'm invited unless you show up."

Ellen nodded. "And when I come for you you'll be there, won't you?"

"I'll be there," Lori said. "That's a promise." She held out her hand, and Ellen shook it to seal their agreement.

"Here's the corner." Lori nudged Doug. "Will you let me out here, mister? I don't want the Stones to know I came in a car."

"I'll let you out if you'll call me Doug."

"Okay, Doug. Will you let me out here?" Lori grinned at him.

Doug slowed the car, then stopped. He slid out, and Lori scrambled after him. "Now drive on," she ordered. "I don't want Mrs. Stone to look down here and see you waiting like I was a little kid or something."

"Better do it," Ellen whispered. "I want her to go back even if it's on her own terms."

Doug got back into the car and eased into the traffic once more. "I feel like a heel leaving the kid standing there on the corner. How do you know she's going back to the Stones? She may change her mind and take off again. I should have given her some money just in case."

"That's a chance we'll have to take," Ellen said. "And I doubt that she would have accepted your money. But Lori and I made a deal. I trust her, Doug. I think she'll keep her word. I think she'll be at the Stones' waiting for me this evening."

"Waiting for *us*," Doug corrected. "I'm in on this too. You could get in big trouble hiding a runaway."

"I haven't been hiding her," Ellen said. "Most of the time I couldn't find her myself. And if I had turned her in, she would have hidden herself with greater care. But let's forget about Lori until this evening. This is my day off, remember?"

"Right. I'm not likely to forget."

"Where is this museum you want me to see?"

Doug turned from the residential streets and headed into the heart of the village. They jounced across railroad tracks, and then he parked the car in the shade of a maple outside the old railroad depot.

"Here it is." Doug took his clipboard and pencil from the dashboard of the car before he got out; then he opened Ellen's door for her. "This museum's not fancy, but it's interesting."

The inside of the depot was not air conditioned, and a small fan hummed on the desk beside a high-school girl who sat reading a paperback mystery. The girl looked up, smiled, then went back to her reading.

Doug wandered to one side of the room to examine an old ice storage bin. Ellen followed him, watching him take a few notes here and there. Doug wrote a brief description of a table bearing a deer design that had been burned into its top by an artist with a hot poker.

" 'This type of art was popular in the early 1900s,' " Ellen read from a display card on the table. "It must have required a steady hand."

In another room they viewed an oak jury chair with curving arms and flat spindles. In a glass case plumes and beaded purses had been preserved for posterity. Ellen noticed that Doug didn't write very much, but he paused before a bamboo easel and a lithograph as if he were trying to memorize them.

"Will you use descriptions of these things in a book?" Ellen asked at last.

"Maybe. Maybe not. I never know for sure

until the time comes. If I need a plumed pen or a beaded watch fob in my story, in they'll go."

"You haven't taken many notes," Ellen said.

"I've never been able to decide if note-taking is a good idea or not," Doug said. "If I need to know details and I have notes on them, I can save a lot of time, but it seems to me that if a thing is important enough to write about, then it should remain crystal clear in my memory."

"Some days I can hardly remember my name." Ellen giggled. "I'm for note-taking."

"Have you seen enough?" Doug asked at last.

"I think so," Ellen said. "I'm glad we came. The maps of the lake area are interesting — even the ones that mark the trail of Inkpaduta and his raiders."

When they were back in the car, Doug headed for a secluded beach on East Okoboji. "We won't have a boat, but we can swim and sunbathe."

They left the car at the side of the road high above the lake and followed rickety wooden steps down to the water. Turning right, Doug led the way to an inlet with a sandy, sun-drenched beach.

"Want to swim first or eat first?" Doug

asked, plunking the picnic basket on a shady knoll near a pine.

"Swim, of course." Ellen grinned. "Remember the old safety rule: no swimming for an hour after eating. It's a wise rule to follow. Of course, if you're starving we could eat first, rest for a while, then swim."

"All right, Nurse." Doug grinned. "I vote for swimming first."

They slipped off the clothes they wore over their swimsuits. Doug splashed into the water, and Ellen followed. A frog splashed in with them. Today there was no raft to race to, so they just swam parallel to the shore until they tired. Then they waded from the water and flopped down on the sand to rest. Doug wasn't as strong a swimmer as Frank, but he seemed to enjoy himself more.

"You really like the water, don't you?" Ellen asked.

Doug nodded. "I had a hard time learning to swim, though. I was almost fifteen before I had any real confidence in myself. And then some kids threw me in and I had to swim or drown. Or so I thought. If it hadn't been for that experience, I might still be a wader who considers swimming a spectator sport."

"Sounds as if you really learned the hard

way. I took Red Cross lessons on Saturday mornings. I've always loved to swim. I'm happy when I'm in the water."

"Swimming and happiness are a lot alike." Doug sat up and began to shape a castle in the sand at his feet.

"How so?"

"At first I fought the water and sank every time I tried to swim," Doug said. "But when those guys threw me in, I knew I had to do something smart. I couldn't trust myself, so I trusted the lake. Once I relaxed, the water buoyed me up. It was a strange wonder to me — one I'll never forget. Same thing with happiness. When I fight for the buoyancy of happiness, I lose it, but when I relax and get interested in something else or someone else, happiness comes along. Right now I'm quite interested in you."

Ellen wanted to smile at Doug's comparison, but she couldn't. She knew he was very serious, and when he grew serious about something, she sensed an unrest in him that troubled her. Doug spoke of serious matters, yet he kept many things hidden below the surface of his talk. He was an enigma.

"How about that lunch?" Ellen asked when Doug's sand castle caved in and melted back into the beach. "I'm starved."

"Okay." Doug smiled once more, and they

walked to the grassy knoll where they had left the picnic basket. Doug spread out a red gingham cloth Josie had packed, and Ellen began to set out the food. Cold fried chicken. Tomato and cucumber salad. Iced chocolate milk. Potato chips. Fresh peaches.

"She thought of everything, didn't she?" Ellen said. "Aunt Madeleine doesn't know how lucky she is to have Josie working for her."

"I think maybe she knows," Doug said. "I think your aunt's gratitude plays a large part in keeping Josie happy. She's not one to work for money alone."

"Don't know what Aunt Madeleine would do without her."

"I've been thinking about that," Doug said. "Did you know that Mr. Boast is a retired businessman?"

"Yes. Frank told me."

"I think there's a chance that he might be persuaded to help your aunt with the lodge," Doug said. "I've been visiting with him quite a bit lately, and he's bored to death with retirement. He feels as if he's going to seed. And he's full of suggestions for improving the lodge."

"I might mention that to Aunt Madeleine," Ellen said. "I think she's ready for some practical help, and she'd be able to check on his credit rating and such. But I'll wait a few days. I've got enough on my mind right now. And in the meantime maybe Mr. Boast will approach the subject himself."

They ate Josie's lunch, and as they ate, Doug told Ellen about his childhood in Kansas, his service in Vietnam, his going to college, dropping out, and returning to earn a diploma with a master's degree in English literature. And Ellen found herself telling Doug about her past, about her parents' being killed in a car accident, about living in foster homes, boarding schools, and college dorms.

"I used to think Aunt Madeleine didn't care enough about me to let me live with her and Uncle Brad," Ellen said. "So I was like Lori; I pretended I could make it on my own. When I grew older I realized that Aunt Madeleine cared too much about me to ask me to live with her. She and Uncle Brad lived a helter-skelter life. Iowa in the summer, Spain in the fall, the South of France in the winter. It was too unstable a life for a child."

When they were all talked out, Ellen began packing the picnic things back into the basket. Doug walked back down to the beach, and when she joined him, he took her in his arms.

"Ellen, will you marry me? I love you very much. I realize that we haven't known each other for very long, but I knew I loved you from that first morning when I met you walking along the shore at Scarlet Point. Don't give me an answer right now. Think it over. But remember, nobody can make it on his own. Everyone needs someone. I need you, and I hope you need me."

Doug kissed her, and when she caught her breath, Ellen backed away and looked at him with a new insight. "I don't know what to say, Doug. I've felt very attracted to you, but I've never believed in love at first sight — or even second or third sight. It's far too soon for me to know whether or not I love you."

"I told you I didn't want an answer right now." Doug put a forefinger against her lips as if to silence her. "Think it over carefully."

"We've known each other so briefly. I don't want to use marriage as a runaway haven as Lori is using Scarlet Point."

"Who says you'd be running away anywhere?" Doug asked. "If you decide to marry me, I'll go with you wherever you want to go. My office is in my hat. I can write here, in California, anywhere. I could write on the moon as long as you were there with me."

"Doug —" Ellen scuffed her toe in the sand. She had been so caught up in Doug's proposal, so carried away, that she had almost forgotten one important thing.

"What's the matter?" Doug asked. "What's troubling you? I can tell there's more bothering you than the briefness of our acquaintance."

"What about Julie Jackson?" Ellen blurted the question and let it sizzle between them.

Doug backed off a step, but his expression never changed. "How did you know about her?"

"I wasn't spying on you. Really I wasn't. But yesterday when I stopped at the lodge desk to pick up my mail I saw a letter for you. I'll admit I was curious. I read the return address. Julie Jackson."

Ellen waited for Doug to explain Julie Jackson to her satisfaction, or at least to say she was a girl from the past who no longer mattered to him. She was willing to believe anything Doug said. She wanted to believe. But Doug said nothing. He seemed neither angry nor upset nor ruffled in any way. But he refused to discuss Julie Jackson.

"Let's go back to the lodge," Doug said. "I know you'll want to freshen up and change clothes before you make an appearance at the Stone home on Lori's behalf."

They said little on the ride back to the lodge, and when they reached the parlor, it was quite by accident that Ellen saw Frank and Janey coming up the steps from the quay. She wouldn't have thought much about it if they hadn't been holding hands and if Frank hadn't had a lipstick smear on his cheek.

CHAPTER FOURTEEN

Ellen showered and changed clothes. She managed to appear at the dinner table. She managed to smile at all the guests, even Frank and Janey and Doug. Everything seemed unreal. She and Doug had just eaten lunch a short time ago. Could it be possible that it was dinner time already? Ellen felt like a robot whose actions had been programmed by a computer. Had Frank really asked her to go with him to New York? Was he really waiting for an answer? Had Doug really asked her to marry him? If so, what about Julie Jackson? Nothing made sense.

After dinner Ellen helped Josie in the kitchen, and so did Doug. How she wished she hadn't asked him about Julie Jackson! Yet she did have a right to know. She didn't want to become emotionally involved with a man who was already emotionally involved with another woman.

And what about Frank and Janey? Ellen tried not to be jealous of Janey. She mustn't be jealous. Jealousy would only make her hospital decision more difficult. She had to be impartial.

"Did you two have a good time on your day off?" Josie smiled at Ellen.

"A very good time." Ellen avoided looking at Doug. "We visited the depot museum, and then we swam in East Okoboji. Your picnic lunch really crowned the day. It was just great."

"Right on," Doug chimed in. "You packed all my favorite things."

Josie chattered as they worked, and when the kitchen was back in order, Ellen tried to slip away without saying any more to Doug. But he caught up with her on the stairs.

"Do you want me to go with you to get Lori? I'll be glad to drive you."

"You don't need to, Doug. I can face the Stones alone."

"But there's no need for you to have to. I'd like to come along. And I think you'll find that it's good to have someone to back you up."

Ellen grinned. "Come along, then." Surely Doug wasn't angry with her about prying into his private life. If he was angry, he wouldn't have volunteered to come along.

191

Maybe Julie Jackson was his cousin.

This time Ellen drove her car. She parked it in front of the Stones' house, and she and Doug walked up to the front porch. Ellen knocked. A short, plump woman appeared at the door immediately. Her ready smile matched her comfortable figure.

"Mrs. Stone?" Ellen asked.

The woman nodded. "Yes, I'm Mrs. Stone. May I help you?"

"I'm Ellen Ferris from Scarlet Point Lodge. Your foster daughter, Lori Wilde, is a friend of mine, and I've come to ask if she may spend the night with me at the lodge. I could bring her back early in the morning."

Mrs. Stone's smile faded. "Are you the friend who's been hiding her?"

"No. Not really. I discovered Lori hiding at the lodge. I didn't call the authorities, but I did encourage her to come back here of her own free will."

Mrs. Stone relaxed a bit. "Lori told us about her friend at the lodge, but she tells us so many tales that it's hard to know which ones to believe."

"Where is Lori?" Ellen asked. "May we see her?"

This time Mrs. Stone sighed. "I'm afraid she's gone again. Disappeared right after supper. I sent her out with the garbage —

192

not that I'm working her to death or anything, mind you. But a child needs to do a
few chores just to make him feel worthwhile
to himself. Lori never came in from dump-
ing the garbage. I've reported to her social
worker, and my husband is out looking for
her right this minute. But he won't find her.
The child is as slippery as quicksilver."

"Didn't Lori tell you that I was coming to
ask her to stay at the lodge tonight?" Ellen
asked.

"No. She never mentioned that." Mrs.
Stone frowned. "Miss Ferris, I think you
should get in touch with Lori's social
worker first thing in the morning. Her name
is Miss Yanter, and her office is at the
courthouse. I'm sure she'll want to talk with
you. All of this is very unusual, you know.
We were kind to Lori. We did our best for
her. Makes a body wonder . . ."

"Thank you for your consideration, Mrs.
Stone. I will get in touch with Miss Yanter
first thing in the morning. And if you see
Lori tonight, will you call me at Scarlet
Point Lodge?"

"I will," Mrs. Stone said. "But I don't
expect to see her."

Doug took Ellen's arm as they left the
Stones' front porch. "Now, don't panic. Lori
can take care of herself."

"But she shouldn't have to. And I'm not going to panic. I just don't understand. Lori promised. We shook hands on it. I trusted her to keep her word."

"Maybe she thought you had forgotten." Doug glanced at his watch. "Maybe we should have set a definite time to come for her. My guess is that she's back at the lodge. Shall we go take a look?"

Ellen climbed back into her car. "I guess we have no other choice. I can't just write her off as a bad deal. I feel so — responsible. But Mrs. Stone is right. Lori is like quicksilver. How can I be responsible for human quicksilver?"

"You're a little like quicksilver yourself," Doug said. "When I try to pin you down, you slip away from me."

Ellen drove quickly through the residential area, back down the main street of Spirit Lake, and then north of town to the lodge. Tonight a whispering breeze wafted clouds in front of the moon. The lodge grounds were a mosaic of light and shadows.

"Where shall we look first?" Ellen dropped her hands from the steering wheel into her lap. "She'll probably be outside somewhere."

Doug got out of the car and opened Ellen's door for her. "Where have you seen her in the past?"

"Around the rowboat. Those willow branches offer an excellent hiding place."

Instead of taking a shortcut through the lodge parlor and out the patio door, Ellen led the way around the outside of the building. Shades were drawn in the unused portions of the lodge, and Ellen imagined the closed windows as sleeping eyes.

"What a huge old place," Ellen said. "Can you imagine this lodge with every room full?"

"Yes, I can." Doug took Ellen's hand. "From what I understand Scarlet Point used to be quite an exclusive spot — away from the hubbub of West Okoboji. I understand that some shipping magnate owned it and operated it as one of his diversified enterprises. When he died, a grandson inherited the lodge and let the business go downhill."

"And then Aunt Madeleine jumped in with both feet and bought a dying enterprise. She must be losing hundreds of dollars every day, Doug."

Doug squeezed Ellen's hand. "I don't think you aunt is measuring the cost in dollars and cents. She's growing older, and she sees a need for a vacation resort for elderly people. I think she has a great idea. What she needs is a business partner, not just an advisor who isn't in residence and who can't see the everyday problems. But she'll realize that. Before dinner this evening I asked Mr. Boast to have a business talk with her. He's a very persuasive person once he gets off the subject of his health."

"We're coming to the willows." Ellen nodded at the graceful green branches that drooped to touch the ground. "Lori? Lori, are you here?"

"You really don't expect her to answer, do you?" Doug asked. "After all, she's a runaway, and she's gone back on her word to you. My guess is that she's wrestling with some mighty deep guilt feelings at this point." Doug strode to the willows, swept back a branch, and peered into the dark sanctuary the trees enclosed.

"Lori? It's Doug. Are you here?"

"We should have brought a flashlight," Ellen said. "It's too dark to see back in there."

"Wait right here and I'll go get one," Doug said. "Be back in a minute."

Doug sprinted toward the lodge steps, and Ellen leaned back against the trunk of an oak. Maybe if she was quiet, Lori would think she was alone and give herself away by some sound or movement. In the distance a coon dog howled. Overhead a screech owl whispered like a crying baby. Off to her left Ellen heard some creature scurry through the tall grass. A muskrat? A raccoon? Perhaps Lori was in danger spending the night outside. Most wild animals were frightened of humans, but Ellen had read stories of rabid skunks and squirrels who attacked humans without provocation.

Ellen tried to squelch her imagination, tried to see the night as Lori saw it. Lori saw only the beauty. When the moon was under a cloud, the lake looked like obsidian, and the sweet, musky scent of the water perfumed the air.

Suddenly Ellen inhaled the sharp odor of spearmint. Her throat tightened. Someone or something had stepped in the clump of the herb that grew near the lodge steps. Surely Doug hadn't had time to get a flashlight and be back already. Ellen strained her eyes to see through the darkness. Then she heard voices.

"New York . . . the big time . . . super opportunities . . ."

"It all sounds absolutely fascinating. But I can't go with you, Frank. My heart is set on finishing nurse's training in California."

Even in the darkness Ellen felt her face flush. She pressed harder against the oak and held her breath lest some telltale sound give her away. Did Frank ask everybody he met to go to New York with him? Was it just one super-big line he threw out to every girl he met? Ellen pressed even closer to the oak, hoping the deep shadows would hide her. How embarrassing if Frank and Janey should discover her hiding there!

After what seemed an eternity Ellen heard the voices fade into the distance, and when the moon peeked from behind the clouds again, she saw two forms walking along the quay, hand in hand. Now they were too far away for her to hear what they were saying.

"Think I'd never get back?"

Ellen jumped at the sound of Doug's whisper. "I didn't see you come down the steps."

"I was sneaky. I heard Frank and his friend when I was at the top of the steps, so I found a footpath down the slope and avoided them. Any sign of Lori?"

"None. There's so much activity out here tonight that she's probably gone into deeper hiding someplace. She told me she had some other spots lined up for emergency use. Or maybe she didn't come here at all."

"Hold the willow branch back and we'll take a thorough look-see." Doug flashed the light into all corners of the willow area. Lori was not there.

"Maybe she's inside the lodge," Doug said. "She easily could have slipped through a door without being seen. There are dozens of rooms she could hide in."

"True. And right now I'm going to hide in the one Aunt Madeleine assigned to me. All of a sudden I'm bushed. It's been a long day, Doug. If Lori's around here, she'll be okay. She knows the lay of this land. And if she isn't around here, there's nothing we can do about it. Surely the police are keeping an eye out for her, too."

"Let's go," Doug agreed. "There's really nothing more we can do."

"Frankly, I feel as if I've been badly used," Ellen said. "I think Lori has made a fool of me right from the start. She had no intention of staying at the Stones'. It was all a ruse to fool me and keep me from turning her in."

They walked up the steps to the lodge, and after Doug kissed Ellen good night, he whispered, "I'm still waiting for your answer. Remember — I love you."

Ellen squeezed Doug's hand and hurried inside and up the stairs. Once in her room she lost no time in preparing for bed, but once she lay between the sheets she couldn't sleep. Perhaps she had mistaken defeat for exhaustion. She felt like a tire with a slow leak, and she tried to analyze her feelings and their cause.

She trusted people. Maybe that was her downfall. Aunt Madeleine had said she was running a lodge, and Ellen had believed her — until she saw Scarlet Point. She had believed that Lori would be waiting for her at the Stones' tonight. She had been ready to believe that Janey Van Allen really wanted and deserved another try at nursing school.

Was there no integrity left in the world? Frank had asked her to go to New York with him, and she had taken him seriously. Had she imagined that he intended to marry her? Obviously she had read a deeper meaning into his words than he had intended. Frank had said nothing about love or marriage. And what about Doug? Doug had asked her to marry him. Doug had told her that he loved her. Yet he had refused to comment on Julie Jackson. If Julie Jackson meant nothing to him, he would have told her so. Cousin? Ha! Julie was undoubtedly an old girl friend.

Suddenly Ellen got out of bed and went to her desk. Frank, Doug, Lori, Janey — all these people were telling her something, telling her a truth she was trying to ignore because she wanted life to be honest and straightforward. But one couldn't wear blinders and wrap oneself in cotton wool. Ellen wondered what cotton wool was. She had heard the expression many times, but when it came right down to mentally picturing cotton wool, she couldn't do it.

Taking a piece of stationery from her desk drawer, Ellen sat down to write a letter. She would have nothing more to do with Lori or Frank or Doug or Janey. She had her principles, and she would live by them in spite of what others thought or did.

Quickly Ellen dashed off a letter to the board of directors at her hospital, asking that Janey Van Allen be expelled for cheating on her final exam. She signed the letter, folded it, and slipped it into an envelope.

Now she felt as if someone had released the rope around her chest that had been restricting her breathing. For once she knew she had done the right thing. The right thing. The right thing. Ellen repeated the words like a chant, wondering why she still couldn't fall asleep.

When the pebbles hit her window screen, Ellen was still wide awake. She hurried to the window and looked down into the yard.

CHAPTER FIFTEEN

Down on the patio below Ellen's window Lori stood, half in shadow, half in moonlight, her cupped hand filled with pebbles. She was just winding up to throw another one when Ellen called down to her.

"Where have you been, Lori? Doug and I searched all over for you."

Now that she had Ellen's attention Lori stared at the concrete and scuffed at some grass growing through a crack. She looked so small and forlorn standing there in the ragged moonlight that Ellen forgot all her anger and disappointment.

"Wait right there, Lori. I'll be down in a jiffy." Ellen slipped into robe and loafers and tiptoed down the stairs to the patio door. The key made a loud scraping in the lock, but nobody stirred. Ellen opened the door and slipped outside, half expecting Lori to have vanished. But Lori was still waiting for her.

Ellen wanted to rush to the child, to throw her arms around her thin shoulders, but she squelched that desire and tried to force some starch into her voice. She wouldn't let Lori use her again.

"I'm disappointed in you, Lori." Immediately Ellen wished she could snatch back those words. How she had hated it as a child when someone had said, "I'm disappointed in you, Ellen." The words had made her feel defeated and selfish and worthless. Yet this was a different situation. As a child she had never promised to do the things the adults were always disappointed in her for not doing. But Lori *had promised.* Ellen had a perfect right to be disappointed. Promises were trusts to be kept. Ellen repeated her words. "I'm disappointed in you, Lori."

"I don't blame you, lady," Lori said.

"Can't you call me Ellen? It's my name. I hate being called 'lady.' "

"Okay, Ellen. I don't like being called 'kid,' either. But that's what the cops always call me. Kid."

"You're trying to change the subject," Ellen said. "Where were you tonight when Doug and I called for you at the Stones'?"

"I didn't think you'd come for me," Lori said. "I didn't want anyone to know I had been dumb enough to trust you. I ran away because I wanted to show everyone that I could make it on my own."

"I know that by this time," Ellen said. She led Lori to a bench, and they sat down in the shadow of the lodge.

"I was hiding right there in the yard all the time you were on the Stones' porch," Lori said.

"But when you saw that I had come for you, why didn't you speak out?"

"I was afraid. I knew Mr. Stone was out searching for me. I knew they had called my social worker."

"That wouldn't have mattered," Ellen said.

"I was ashamed. I was ashamed to admit that you had trusted me but that I hadn't trusted you. Everyone needs someone to trust them." All at once Lori began crying — not just sniveling, but crying in great racking sobs. Ellen put her arm around her and patted her shoulder. How could she have misjudged Lori so?

"Come on upstairs with me, Lori. You can sleep in my room tonight. I've got a great big bed that's plenty large enough for both of us."

To Ellen's surprise Lori came willingly. She stifled her sobs, and holding Ellen's hand, she tiptoed up the stairs and didn't say a word until the bedroom door was closed behind them.

"Do you think the cops are looking for me?" Lori asked.

"I just think they might be. And if they come here and find you, I could be in big trouble. We'd both have a lot of explaining to do."

"You'd risk getting into big trouble for me?" Lori asked.

"I guess you'd be worth it." Ellen smiled at Lori and gave her a pajama top to wear to bed.

"I sleep in my clothes." Lori laid the pajama top aside. "Pajamas are for sissies."

Ellen shrugged. "Hope you don't mind sleeping with a sissy."

"I don't." Lori grinned at Ellen and tucked her transistor under her pillow.

"Are you hungry?" Ellen asked.

"No."

"Thirsty?"

"No."

"Need to go to the bathroom?"

"For cripes sake, you sound like Mrs. Stone. I'm fine. Superduper okay. I can take care of myself."

Ellen snapped off the light and crawled into bed beside Lori. Lori clung to the outer edge of the mattress as if she were afraid she might touch Ellen. She twitched and squirmed for a while; then she lay quietly, but Ellen could tell by Lori's uneven breathing that she wasn't asleep.

"Something bothering you?" Ellen asked at last.

"One little thing," Lori said. "Tomorrow morning I want to go back to the Stones'."

"I sort of had that in mind," Ellen said. "You're going to have to face the Stones. And there's a Miss Yanter — the social worker. And maybe the police."

"I don't care about Miss Yanter and the cops. But I want to go back to the Stones'. Grandmother Stone needs me to read to her. Nobody else has the time but me."

"I'll see that you get back first thing in the morning. Even before breakfast."

Again Ellen lay quietly for a while, and this time Lori soon fell asleep. When Ellen felt it was safe, she slipped downstairs to a telephone and called Mrs. Stone. She told her that Lori was safe and that she would return her early in the morning. No use letting people worry needlessly.

Why couldn't she fall asleep? Ellen wondered as she lay in bed once more. But she knew why. Her thoughts were like Ping-Pong balls bouncing from Lori to Doug to

Frank to Janey. If she had misjudged Lori, perhaps she had misjudged the others, too. Everyone had special reasons for their actions that made sense to them.

Slipping from bed once again, Ellen paced, and as she paced she tried to muddle out where she had gone wrong in her dealings with the people at Scarlet Point. Where had she gone wrong, and what could she do about it? She paused at her window, and a movement below caught her eye. In the shadows of the pines Frank was giving Janey a good-night kiss.

Ellen turned away. That did it! She might have misjudged Lori Wilde, but surely she had been right about the others. In her mind she began to see Frank more clearly.

Frank expected some special place in the world to make him famous. But so far he had always worked for somebody else. Nobody knew his name as an architect. Ellen suspected that Frank was working backwards. If he ever succeeded in his career, it would be because he had done all he could to improve a certain area.

Ellen felt all jealousy of Janey vanish. Tomorrow morning she would tell Frank that she definitely wasn't going to New York with him. Not that he would care. She would tell Doug that she wasn't ready for marriage. And she would tell Janey her decision about the cheating. With no thought of waking Lori, Ellen snapped on her desk lamp, picked up the letter she had written to the hospital board, and addressed and stamped the envelope.

Ellen was still lying in bed wide awake an hour later. Only the fact that Lori was sleeping kept her from tossing and turning and tugging at the covers. At first she thought she imagined that she smelled smoke. She sniffed, and smelled nothing except the pungent lake breeze wafting through the window. Then she inhaled again. There was no mistake. She smelled smoke.

Surely Aunt Madeleine had learned her lesson about flues and fireplaces! Ellen jumped up. She snapped on the desk lamp, and when her eyes adjusted to the light, she saw black smoke wisping through the crack above her bedroom door. Her first impulse was to open the door, but some inner voice warned her. She touched the wood with her fingertips, then jerked her hand away quickly. The door was red hot.

"Lori!" Ellen ran to the bed and shook Lori by the shoulder. "Lori! Wake up. I think the lodge is on fire."

Lori sat up, sleepy eyed; then she began to cough as the smoke grew thicker in the room. Ellen snatched a shirt from her closet and wedged it into the crack above the door. She tucked a pair of slacks into the crack below the door.

"Can't we run downstairs?" Lori asked.

Ellen shook her head. "The door is hot. That means the fire is right outside in the hallway somewhere. Take a shoe and bang on the floor to wake up the others. Bang on the walls. I'll call the fire department."

At the time Ellen had asked her aunt for a private telephone she had felt a bit guilty and thought it an extravagance. But now she knew it was one of the smarter things she had done in her few days at Scarlet Point. Quickly she found the emergency number and dialed.

"Fire department," the crisp voice answered.

"This is Ellen Ferris at Scarlet Point. The lodge is on fire. Please send help quickly."

"Right."

Ellen replaced the receiver, not waiting to hear more. Lori was pounding on the floor so loudly that Ellen had to shout to make her hear.

"We have to get out of here, Lori. You can stop pounding now. I think everyone has surely heard." By now the bedroom was so full of smoke that Ellen's eyes were streaming and she could hardly move about for coughing and choking. Lori was spluttering, and she began to cry.

"Stop that," Ellen ordered. "You're going to need every bit of your energy and your courage. Lie on the floor."

"What if the flame bursts through that door?" Lori asked. "I'm scared."

"Lie down. Right now." Ellen avoided the question that was uppermost in her mind, too. She poured water from the carafe on her nightstand onto a pillowcase and handed it to Lori.

"Wrap this around your head and lie on the floor. Do it. This minute. There's sometimes a pocket of clear air near the floor."

Lori obeyed, placing the soaked pillowcase over her head. Ellen soaked the other pillowcase and tried to hold it over her own face as she stripped the sheets from the bed. I've seen this done in movies, she thought.

"What are you doing?" Lori asked. "Why don't we jump out the window before it's too late?"

"Because you'll break your bones jumping so far." Ellen coughed and spluttered. "We'll try my idea first. If it fails, we may have to jump." She lay down on the floor, keeping her head close to the carpet as she tied the two sheets together with a square knot she had learned to make years ago at one of the summer camps Aunt Madeleine had sent her to.

Crawling on her stomach, Ellen knotted one end of the sheet-rope to the head of the bed. Then she dragged the bed across the floor until it stood in front of the window.

"Now, Lori. Get up. Now's your chance to show me how well you can take care of yourself. I want you to climb down these sheets. They'll hold you. They don't reach to the ground, but you can jump that last little ways."

Tossing the wet pillowcase aside, Lori climbed to the window ledge and looked down. Then she turned back into the room. "I can't do it, Ellen. I can't. I'm afraid."

"You've got to. We're both going to have to be brave and get ourselves out of here."

"You called the fire department," Lori said. "I heard you. Let's wait until the fire engine gets here. The firemen'll rescue us."

"We can't wait that long." Ellen glanced over her shoulder at the door. The paint on the inside was rising in rough bubbles the size of a fingernail. "Go on, Lori. You've always been able to take care of yourself. Now's the time to really prove it. Think how proud of you your mother will be."

Lori balanced on the window ledge on her

stomach. "I can't do it."

"I'll hold you," Ellen promised. She leaned out the window, barely conscious of Judge Cloud and Miss Speer below her on the patio. "I'll hold you, Lori. I'll hold you until you get a hand grip on the sheets. Then just let yourself down hand over hand. Wrap your legs around the sheet so you don't go too fast."

Lori closed her eyes and nodded. Ellen thought Lori's weight would pull her arms from their sockets before the child gripped the sheets and supported herself. Now Lori was on the outside of the lodge, but again she stalled.

Ellen felt heat against her legs, and she heard a crackling sound. Looking over her shoulder, she saw that tongues of flame had burned through the door and were now licking across the carpet.

"Lori, go on," Ellen urged. "Let go with one hand at a time. Hold yourself with your legs until you get another handhold, but *go on.* The fire is right in the room now."

"I can't. I can't," Lori wailed and clung to the sheet, blocking Ellen's descent from the window.

CHAPTER SIXTEEN

Ellen remembered having heard that a drowning person relived his whole life in a few moments before death. Now, with the flames fast approaching, the events of the past week flashed through her mind. But instead of feeling remorse, she felt elation. Happenings that at the time had seemed frightening and frustrating now fell into a meaningful pattern. She felt like the great artist Renoir must have felt at the end of his life when he said, "At last I am beginning to understand." At last she was beginning to understand. At last she could make sense of things. But perhaps the understanding had come too late.

As the flames crept closer, Ellen perched on the window ledge, leaned toward Lori, and forcibly unclenched one of the child's hands from the folds of the sheet.

"Now grab hold lower down," Ellen commanded. "Do it, Lori."

Lori slipped a few feet down the sheet but caught hold again. Now Ellen had room to start down the makeshift rope. Would the sheets support both of them? She couldn't risk it. Unable to reach Lori's hands a second time, Ellen could only call encouragement. Somehow letting go once gave Lori courage to do it again. Now she was going hand over hand. Slowly. But she was going down.

"I've got her," Mr. Boast called up to Ellen. "Now you come. Quickly."

With the flames licking higher and higher in the room Ellen lost no time in obeying. She scraped her knee on the side of the lodge, and she slipped down the sheets so quickly that she felt the fabric searing her hands. But she was down. A miracle! She was safe.

"Where's Aunt Madeleine?" Ellen asked, clutching Lori to her and staring at the guests who had had no trouble getting out of their first-floor rooms. "And Doug? And Janey? Frank? Where is everyone?"

Judge Cloud appeared at her side, leading Aunt Madeleine, who wept hysterically. The judge pointed upward, and Ellen looked. Janey was descending from the second floor using a sheet-rope just as she and Lori had done, but Frank and Doug were sitting on the windowsills of their rooms.

"Are you all right?" Ellen called.

"Trapped in here, but okay so far," Doug answered.

"Use the sheets," Ellen shouted. "Make a rope."

"Tried," Doug called. "Sheets were too old. They ripped."

Ellen felt her heart pounding like a drum. Where was the fire department? She glanced at her watch. Only a few minutes had passed since she had made her emergency call — it just seemed like hours. Then in the distance Ellen heard the wailing sirens.

"Hang on, guys," Ellen shouted. "They're coming. The fire department is on its way."

When the fire trucks arrived, the firemen hooked a hose to the hydrant in front of the lodge and began fighting the flames. Two firemen brought a ladder to the back side of the lodge, and Doug and Frank quickly climbed down to safety.

"Is everyone out?" a fireman asked.

Ellen counted heads. "Yes. Everyone's out."

"But can you save the lodge?" Mr. Boast asked. "I've promised Mrs. Ferris to be her business partner. I hope there's a business left to partner."

"We're doing our best, sir. We'll save the

lodge if we can."

Two hours later the firemen pronounced the blaze under control. Hospital attendants arrived in an ambulance and took Aunt Madeleine and the older guests to the hospital for checkups and for housing for the rest of the night.

Once the fire was under control it was easy to see that only a small part of the vast lodge had been damaged. Ellen managed to find bedding, and she made up beds in another wing for temporary use that night. Doug helped, and after Frank and Janey and Lori were settled for the night, Doug and Ellen sat down on the patio, exhausted.

"What do you think caused the blaze?" Ellen asked. "Did Aunt Madeleine pull another foolish trick? Did she leave a fireplace blaze smoldering or something? It was rather cool last evening."

"I don't think we can blame your aunt this time." Doug wiped soot from his face. "I was talking to the fire chief. He thinks faulty wiring caused the fire. Your aunt may have to close the lodge for a week or so until she can shift her base of operation to a different wing of the structure. But the lodge can be repaired. No permanent harm has been done."

"I'm going for a walk, Doug. I know I'll

never be able to sleep with that smoky smell wafting about. I can still hear those flames. I can still see Lori's panic-stricken look as she tried to climb down those sheets. I may never be able to sleep again."

Doug rose and followed Ellen down to the water. "Mind if I tag along? I'm sure I won't be able to sleep, either."

They walked in silence, and Ellen reconsidered the thoughts that had come to her during the fire. She was hardly aware that Doug was with her until she was ready to speak to him. Then, turning, she was almost surprised to find him at her elbow.

"Doug, I've reached a decision." Ellen looked deep into Doug's eyes. "I'd like to accept your proposal of marriage — if the offer's still open, that is. I think I've loved you ever since that first morning I saw you with your clipboard and pencil and your David Copperfield look."

"David Cooperfield look?"

"The 'I'm starved, please feed me' look." Ellen laughed, knowing she must sound crazy to Doug.

"You've flipped, girl. But I'll accept your acceptance before you come to your senses." Doug kissed Ellen, and she forgot all about the smoky smell that clung to them, that hung all about them.

"I have something to show you." Doug reached into the pocket of his jeans.

For a moment Ellen half expected him to come up with an engagement ring. Yet he wouuldn't have bought a ring not knowing what her answer would be. She was surprised when he held a piece of paper toward her.

"Read this."

"What is it?"

"Read it and see."

Ellen unfolded the slip of paper and read half to herself and half aloud.

Mr. Douglas Cooper
Scarlet Point Lodge
Spirit Lake, Iowa

Dear Mr. Cooper:

It is with pleasure that I inform you that the Braddox Publishing Company has decided to publish your novel, NO TRUMPETS, NO DRUMS. Advance payment will be $2000, half payable on signing of the contract and the other half payable on receipt of the completed script. You will receive a standard 10% royalty on the first 10,000 copies and 15% on additional sales. I hope these terms are agreeable to you.

I am returning the script under separate cover along with suggestions for minor revisions.

Sincerely,
Julie Jackson, Editor

"Doug! How wonderful! Congratulations!" Ellen scanned the letter again before she returned it to Doug. "Why didn't you tell me sooner? Why didn't you tell me about the sale — and about Julie Jackson?"

"Guess I wanted to know if you loved me for myself alone, if you had faith that someday I would have a book published. And I guess I wanted to know if I really trusted you, trusted you to see beyond the blue jeans and the clipboard to whatever there is underneath."

"A few days ago I might not have deserved that trust," Ellen said. "But I think that during these trying times at Scarlet Point I've earned it. Or maybe it's just trust in myself that I've earned. I'm going back to California, Doug. I'm going to compromise and ask the hospital board to allow Janey to continue her training on the condition that she keeps her record clean from now on. I feel that expelling her would do more harm than good. Of course, that request will come after I've asked the board to change my name to Mrs. Douglas Cooper."

Doug pulled Ellen down on the quay beside him, and they dangled their feet in the water, shoes and all.

"I've always felt that every prudent act is based on compromise," Doug said. "But do you mind telling me how you reached that decision?"

"I wish I could say by the use of my brain, but if I said that, I'd be lying. I can hardly explain. I feel as if I've *lived* the answers. Does that make sense? I suppose not. But everything seemed clear to me while I was trapped in that burning room. I knew then what I had to do."

Ellen sighed and leaned into the curve of Doug's arm. "I've been observing Aunt Madeleine trying to function in a capacity that is totally foreign to her. That's the way I'd be if I tried to do anything but teach nursing. Then I observed Josie being so competent in her chosen field. Everyone has a niche in life. Josie has found hers, and I've found mine. And I think Janey has found hers."

"Mr. Boast is going to help your aunt, Ellen. I think that working together they'll make an efficient team. But go on. I didn't mean to interrupt."

"When that speedboat swamped Frank's

canoe, I learned that it doesn't do any good to have the right-of-way if you're destroyed in the process of being right. And a storm that breaks the sturdy oaks, which stand firm against it, only bends the willows, which bow to the blast and live to see another day."

"I think you've made the right decision," Doug said.

"You certainly didn't help me out when I told you my problem and asked your opinion."

"That was intentional. I wanted you to solve your difficulties on your own. I wanted you to be like Lori and do the brave thing."

"My whole life has been built on compromises," Ellen said, "and all in all it's been a good life. I've few complaints. I compromised on going into nurse's training; then I found I could do additional work that would qualify me for teaching nursing. If I had gone my own stubborn way, I probably would never have made it through school."

"I think it was Ibsen who said that the man is in the right who is most closely in league with the future. That's you, Ellen — you're in league with the future. And I'm proud to be a part of that future."

Exhaustion finally overcame Ellen, and she allowed Doug to walk her to her new room. She fell onto the bed without even spreading out the sheets. As she fell asleep she had no regrets. She was glad that Frank and Janey had become close friends. Frank was smooth. He reminded her of West Okoboji Lake. Doug was like Big Spirit. In her heart Ellen knew that Doug would always be a restless person. He would always be churning deep under the surface of life, searching for that elusive something that might be truth. But Ellen wouldn't have it any other way. From the beginning of her stay at Scarlet Point Lodge Big Spirit had fascinated her much more than West Okoboji.

Ellen turned over and thought of decision-making events that she had forgotten to mention to Doug. Lori Wilde. Lori reminded her so much of herself a decade ago that it was almost frightening. In meeting Lori she had met herself and been reminded that everyone needs someone, no matter how hard they protest that it isn't true. Lori would have the Stones. Aunt Madeleine would have Mr. Boast. How lucky she was to have Doug!

Now, as the sun was rising, Ellen relaxed and drifted to sleep.

We hope you have enjoyed this Large Print book. Other Thorndike, Wheeler, and Chivers Press Large Print books are available at your library or directly from the publishers.

For information about current and upcoming titles, please call or write, without obligation, to:

Publisher
Thorndike Press
295 Kennedy Memorial Drive
Waterville, ME 04901
Tel. (800) 223-1244

or visit our Web site at:

www.gale.com/thorndike
www.gale.com/wheeler

OR

Chivers Large Print
published by BBC Audiobooks Ltd
St James House, The Square
Lower Bristol Road
Bath BA2 3SB
England
Tel. +44(0) 800 136919
email: bbcaudiobooks@bbc.co.uk
www.bbcaudiobooks.co.uk

All our Large Print titles are designed for easy reading, and all our books are made to last.